DISCOVERING
THE
Covering

Becka,

I hope you enjoy this book!
Congratulations on the new baby!
Blessings to you all!

Shamika

Praise For

Discovering the Covering

"THERE ARE NO negatives about this book; like none, not even one. . . There are so many profound things to draw on in this amazing book — faith, love, compassion, forgiveness and change — only to name a few. So many people will find either themselves, friends, family, neighbors, their past and future selves and so much more in this book."

- Kemone Brown, Editor Tamarind Hill Press, United Kingdom

"HIDDEN BENEATH THE grit and suspense, there are deep-rooted emotions, real world problems, and unshakeable faith. I applaud the Author for this eye-opening read."

- Whitney, Lifestyle of the Blessed Bookworm

Discovering
THE
Covering

SHAMICKA C. TONEY

ABSOLUTE AUTHOR PUBLISHING HOUSE

Absolute Author
Publishing House

Unless otherwise noted, Scripture quotations are taken from the Holy Bible, NKJV – New King James Version®. Copyright © 1979, 1980, 1982, 2011 by Thomas Nelson.TM The "NKJV" and "New King James Version" are trademarks registered in the United States Patent and Trademark Office.

Publisher: Absolute Author Publishing House

Project Editor: Tamarind Hill Press

LIBRARY OF CONGRESS FILE CONTROL NUMBER: 1-8046802401

ISBN: 978-1-951028-09-1 (Paperback)
ISBN: 978-1-951028-11-4 (eBook)

PRINTED IN THE UNITED STATES OF AMERICA

Special Thanks

To God

THANK YOU FOR not letting me rest until I completed this book. I started working on this back in 2003. Life got in the way. Years later, I started writing again. Then, doubt got in the way. I intentionally stopped writing out of fear of failure and avoided completing the book because I was afraid. Thank you for keeping me. Thank you for quieting my fears. Thank you for pushing me back to the keyboards. I am so excited for the blessings that are sure to come from this story.

To Meech, Jymil, Tyler & Deshon:

THANK YOU FOR giving me the space and time to develop these amazing characters and to tell their stories. Your sacrifice has allowed me to create something truly special! I love you so much!!

To my friends and family:

THANK YOU FOR your support and encouragement. Your belief in and excitement about this project, helped pull me across the finish line. Mom and Dad, there aren't enough words. I love you so much.

To my Beta Readers:

Whitney Baer — I can't thank you enough for your in-depth feedback, feedback on pacing, prompts and thoughtful insights. Your questions made me dig deeper. *Megan Szep* — Your perspective on my character development and eagle-eying the minute details were invaluable! Your help ensured that my timelines were correct and that all of these characters got the love and attention they deserved. *Kingsley Okechukwu* — I am so thankful for the tough love and your gentle insistence that I write harder and better. Your constructive feedback and spot-on suggestions helped me deliver an amazing story!

CHAPTER 1:
In a Word – FAVORED

*T*HE WORLD SLOWLY started coming into view. She groggily surveyed her surroundings, eventually finding her alarm clock quietly perched on the corner of her nightstand.

Amia was still trying to wake from her slumber when she was confounded by the numbers on the display. Her eyes popped wide open as she threw the covers off.

"That can't be right. How can it be 8:45?"

As Amia struggled to free her toes from the final covers and comprehend how she'd overslept, she reminded herself why the expensive, black-out drapes were so overrated. And why didn't the dang alarm go off? The glare she shot in that direction could have melted the polar ice caps. At that very moment, she vowed that the sleek black timer with its big red digital display had seen its last morning at 2658 Windber Ave.

"Focus Amia," she scolded herself. "Call the office let them know you'll be there soon."

With that, Amia lunged across her bed and grabbed the phone. As she hit the speed-dial and headed towards her closet, she knew she was in for some ragging from Janel — the firm's receptionist. She shook her head thinking about how unique that woman was. Without a doubt, Janel was easily the most interesting combination of sweetie pie meets "whoop that ass" Amia had ever seen. She also knew she was in for some ribbing about how much sparkling cider she'd consumed at yesterday's going-away party for Romero.

"Hold up, Amia. That party was . . ."

She laughed, pressing the off button on the phone. "Oh good Lord, girl! It's Saturday. That would explain why the alarm didn't go off."

Relieved, Amia sighed and laughed at herself as she exited the spacious walk-in closet and flopped back down on the king-sized pillow-top pulling her previously strewn covers back up over her shoulders. She then remembered that she'd blasted her normally reliable wake-up companion. "My bad, Mr. Alarm Clock. You can stay."

Again cozy in her bed, Amia thanked the Lord for protection through the night and for allowing her to see another day. After asking Him for strength to endure whatever may come, she stretched lazily while contemplating whether to get up or catch a few more Z's. Amia weighed the pros and cons of each as she slinked back into the coziness.

She really needed to hit the gym. Her week had been filled with a multitude of excuses for skipping workouts. Then there was the dry cleaners, groceries and a stop by Macy's since their twenty-four-hour sale would be ending at 6 o'clock.

Amia half moaned while contemplating the laundry list of errands that were defining her life this weekend. There had to be at least one thing she could push off . . .

"If I spritz the blouse with perfume, I might be able to get in another wear."

Then, hopping quickly out of bed for the second time in two minutes, she grabbed the multi-colored satin piece, "Yup, I can definitely get away with that," she surmised after taking a full whiff of the shirt's armpits and sliding it back onto the hanger.

"One down."

Though Mia really didn't need anything from Macy's, there wasn't a remote possibility that she'd miss their fifty percent discount offer. After all, everything feels better when it's half price, right?

Mia quickly devised a strategy. She'd hit the Macy's at Ross Park. It was farther away, but she could workout at the gym across the street and because both were near the newly opened Farmer's Market, she'd grab groceries while there.

"Yes girl!" Amia complimented herself on yet another creative compromise – a skill that had been sharpened during her stint as an at-risk youth counselor. In fact, she had been the 'go-to' person whenever there was an exceptionally difficult juvenile. When the others had tried every tactic in the book and found themselves making little leeway, the team would call in their big-gun – and Amia never failed to deliver. Besides, she had a personal connection with those kids.

Amia's younger brother, Jamari, had actually been one of them. "Bad for no reason," some would say. Jamari routinely terrorized his younger siblings with his unruliness and outright refused to listen. At age thirteen, his temper, bad attitude, and total lack of respect had earned him an eviction from their mother's home.

Amia shook her head softly while recalling that conversation with her mother just over ten years ago.

"You know what, Mia," said her exasperated mom. Her voice teeming with resignation.

"I'm sending his hoodlum-wanna-be ass off to Juvie and he can stay there as far as I'm concerned. I've tried talking to him. I've tried extra chores and even punishment. Nothing has worked. I've tried and I've tried and I'm tired. I can't do anything with Jamari anymore. The kids are afraid of him. Your father is out of the country, so I can't send Jamari to him.

"It's so bad that I've got his Parole Officer's number on speed dial. Truth be told, I just told the PO to contact the Judge. His skinny ass is leaving next Friday."

Amia's heart smiled. So much had transpired in the years since that fateful conversation. Her eyes turned towards the grouping of picture frames lovingly displayed on her dresser. With the busyness of her life, Amia hadn't really taken time to appreciate the memories they held since artfully arranging them years earlier. Sure, she'd glanced at the smiling photos while quickly dusting, but she'd never really paused to reflect until now.

Her gaze landed on a smiling photo of herself standing in front of a newly purchased townhome. She tenderly traced the sparkly silver frame while gazing at her younger self. The photo had been taken moments before interviewing for her dream job. Her nervous excitement frozen in time. Amia lifted the picture grinning warmly as her mind traveled back in time.

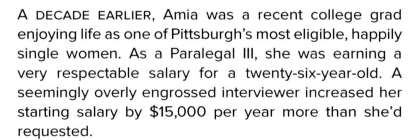

A DECADE EARLIER, Amia was a recent college grad enjoying life as one of Pittsburgh's most eligible, happily single women. As a Paralegal III, she was earning a very respectable salary for a twenty-six-year-old. A seemingly overly engrossed interviewer increased her starting salary by $15,000 per year more than she'd requested.

She couldn't contain her excitement, even taking a

picture while leaping for joy to memorialize the moment. After giddily skipping into her new townhome's foyer, Amia grabbed the phone. Ever the Daddy's girl, all news – good and bad – was shared with Ramon first and that day was no different. But as always, after speaking with her doting dad, she was on the phone with her mom, Elaine.

"Guess what? Yessssss! I got the job! I know. I am so excited."

"What did your Dad say," asked Elaine.

"Mom, maybe I called you first this time," said Amia.

"If you had, it would have been all over the nightly news," replied Elaine.

"I know you've already spoken to Ramon."

"Ok Mom. Yes, I just hung up with Dad," Mia conceded gleefully. "Oh my God, Mom. Tell me why my lucky bra's strap broke in the waiting room five minutes before the interview. Yes, I'm serious. I knew it was on its last leg, but – "

"Umm, is that the same 'lucky bra' that you bought in high school?"

"Yes, Ma'am. I won the lead role in "Birds Like Us" in that bra and it's the one I was wearing when I got the warning instead of that $225.00 speeding ticket. Aaannnd I was even wearing that bra when Brian, Coach Thomas' four-year-old, fell off the bridge and into the river at the picnic. That old bra held up even through my jumping in and dragging him onto the riverbank. Of course I had to wear it yesterday," she added smiling.

"You are unbelievable. I can't believe you still have that old thing. So, did you end up tying the strap in a knot?"

"No. I actually hit it off with this lady who works there named Janel and I asked her if she had a safety pin. I told her why and she actually went to the bathroom with me and pinned the strap back together. I still can't believe it. I was literally just sitting there rehearsing my answers and pop!" Mia laughed.

"Maybe that's why you got the job. She probably told them that your pitiful ass couldn't even afford a damn bra."

Both ladies laughed hysterically at that one. That was one thing Mia adored about her mother. She was super witty and her comedic timing was unmatched.

"Ok Ma, the bra is officially retired as of today. Notice, I said retired. I'm not throwing it away... OK, I love you too. See you this weekend."

By the time Mia and Elaine disconnected, she'd stripped out of her jeans and into her favorite long pale purple T-shirt. She grabbed her half-eaten pint of Ben & Jerry's and flopped down on her couch to review the past twenty-four hours.

While she felt that the dialogue during the interview had gone well, Amia hoped that the job offer and subsequent salary increase were due to her interviewing skills and impressive resume and not her Christian Dior button-down pants suit that had been specifically tailored to her tall, sized twelve frame. The 'power suit' had been given to her as a graduation gift from Ramon. For that particular interview, she opted to pair the navy, penn-striped two-piece with an amber blouse. Mia's goal was to have the double-breasted ensemble reflect her confidence, determination, and elegance — though it didn't hurt that the silk blouse complemented her flawless skin and rose-toned lipstick.

From day one at the firm, it was apparent that Mia would not let the company down. Within nine months, the office was working and winning more cases simply because of Mia's dedication to research and justice.

The partners just won a high profile, media-racked embezzlement case that was deemed a loss from the start. After Amia found similar records of past embezzlement complaints on a recently departed key financial officer of their client's company, the State's previously air-tight case began to leak.

That discovery was followed by more inconsistencies. Amia's hunch about a witness' statement revealed a witness-tampering claim against the investigating officers. With every new finding, there was a new fissure. Glimmers of optimism seeped ever more into the defense team's psyche. Mia's persistence had swung the case from a guaranteed loser to one with a very real possibility of an acquittal.

The Washington, Worthy & Meyer's Law Firm took the case on as a favor to the State's banking institutions. Its astute partners considered it an investment — after all, this case and its notoriety would exponentially increase their national footprint.

After the jury returned an acquittal, they'd hit the town hard in high-celebrity fashion — limos, Dom Perignon, glitz and glam. That evening was spent basking the victory, smiling for the relentless paparazzi, and congratulating everyone on a job well done.

The firm had three partners, one of which was Marty Worthy, the partner who'd hired and increased Mia's pay so tremendously. He'd made it his duty to see that Mia was successful in all she endeavored — both in her career and her personal life. Marty had taken Mia under his wing and it was no secret that he thought of Mia as one of his daughters. Truth be told, Mia could have passed for one of his children. Besides similar thick, curly hair, Mia was tall like him at 5'10" and they each possessed a certain radiance that made them easy to spot in a crowd.

During the celebration party that evening, Marty gave a toast to the staff and concluded with thoughts of adoration and respect for the young lady who he'd known would make a difference at WW&M and impact the lives of everyone whose path she'd been fortunate enough to cross.

Mia and Marty shared a special bond that went far beyond the world of legalities. She smiled as she reminisced about a clear, January morning a year earlier. The pair decided to review upcoming case notes over lunch. As they left the corner bistro and the comfort of its outdoor heated awnings, Mia dutifully recapped her takeaways and next steps. The two continued chatting turning the discussion from work to their weekend plans, when Marty screamed.

"Amia! Amia watch out!" She'd just hustled back into the crosswalk to grab her hat that had been blown off by the wind. Amia heard his scream, but it was too late. She looked up and to her horror, saw a City Transit Bus barreling towards her. It was close enough that she could see the equally horrified eyes of the driver who'd been futilely trying to gain control of the vehicle. Fearing for the worst, Mia braced for impact. A split second later, she was flying backwards. Not from the impact of the massive vehicle, but from the force of Marty's grip. His snatch so powerful that they both ended up face down on the frozen, cracked grey pavement.

"Amia, are you OK," he asked as he helped her up and gathered her strewn belongings.

"Yes, thank you," she replied while dabbing her bleeding forehead and shaking the ache growing in her ankle. Mia hobbled to pick up Marty's broken glasses then they stared in disbelief at the mangled remains of what had been a shiny blue Grand Cherokee only a few seconds earlier. The bus had hit black ice at 45 miles an hour destroying the vehicle before crashing into a storefront injuring thirteen passengers.

Amia stared at the mangled carnage absorbing the magnitude. The cries of the injured escaped through the shattered buses' windows. Lunch-time patrons abandoned their steaming meals to become rescuers. Sirens began echoing off of the cold grey buildings. A solitary tear streamed down Amia's face.

"Amia? Are you ok," asked Marty.

"I . . ." she whispered with the realization that she'd escaped death.

"You saved my life."

Marty in his now tattered winter coat, helped her into a nearby deli where they picked salt pellets from their clothes and hair while talking about her near-death experience. As a devout Christian, Marty couldn't let the moment pass without asking her if she was saved. It was that afternoon, while still shaking off the shock and nursing her sprained ankle, that Marty saved her life again by leading her to salvation.

Up until that moment, Mia was the typical, invincible twenty-six-year-old who knew she'd live forever and really didn't see a need for God. After all, she'd gotten this far all by herself — hadn't she? Mia wiped a tear as she reminisced about that day at the café where she and Marty prayed, and she gave her life to the Lord.

Just then she was jolted back to reality by thunderous clapping and chants of "speech, speech, speech, speech."

Mia thanked all the partners, attorneys, paralegals, secretaries, work-study students, and especially Marty for everything. She was too humble to accept all of their accolades without assuring her counterparts that it was God who'd done it. She told them all that she just enjoyed being the person that He'd used.

Marty looked like a father who'd just seen his daughter in her wedding dress. He was in awe at the wisdom, wonderful spirit, and beauty that this woman possessed and exuded. Not five minutes after giving her impromptu speech, Mia's cell phone began buzzing. It was Jamari.

Mia excused herself from the party and tried desperately to listen to her little brother who was barely audible due to his intense crying. Jamari was so distraught that he couldn't catch his breath, let alone tell Mia what was wrong.

"Mari, did something happen to Mom or Dad?"

"No."

"Bria, Jordyn, or Shamir?"

"Nooooo," was all he could manage before resuming his profuse sobbing.

Having confirmed that her parents and siblings were all fine, Mia knew that he'd probably gotten into trouble again. Only this time, she knew that whatever happened was a game-changer.

CHAPTER 2:
In a Word – MOTIVATION

"THINK MIA, THINK," she implored herself recognizing that she had to come up with something to calm him down to have any hopes of getting to the bottom of Jamari's woes. Mia began to tell him about the victory celebration and talk about the Paparazzi stationed outside their suite. Fascinated, Jamari relaxed momentarily and began asking her additional questions about the party and told her that he'd seen her on TV walking out of the courtroom.

After a few minutes, Mia was satisfied that he'd chilled out enough to speak, so she asked her little brother what happened.

"Mom is sending me off to Juvie, Yo. I'm 'bout to be there til I'm 18. Mia, I don't wanna go." He stumbled with his words because he began crying intensely again. "I told her I was sorry, Mia. I don't wanna gooooo..."

Mia didn't hear anything else. Jamari was no longer speaking – at least not coherently. Words were mottled by his sobbing and had he not been her brother, she'd never have believed she was speaking to a teenager as his weeping was so uncontrollable.

"Hang on a second Mari." Mia hurried back into the celebration and asked everyone to forgive her early departure. Marty shot her a concerned look to which she mouthed, "I'll tell you later." Mia threw fake smiles at the paparazzi who couldn't get enough of her in the kelly-green asymmetrical dress that she'd stumbled on a few months earlier while looking for a new workout top. The dress was 'hidden' on the rack by a hopeful owner who'd expected to return and purchase the only one left. Mia decided that she'd keep her current exercise wardrobe and opted to take the gorgeous gown home with her. She'd never had an opportunity to let the shimmery number drape around her curves until tonight.

Mia had taken her curls down while waiting for her car and both her hair and dress were now being playfully ruffled by the ever-cooling evening breeze. While she tried not to pay too much attention to the photogs, deep down, she hoped the pictures would look as good as she felt. She even angled her body so that they could capture her best side all the while making idle chitchat with Jamari to avoid suspicion.

Once in the solitude of her vehicle, Mia assured Mari that he would not be going away. Mari told Mia earlier in their conversation that their mom was working late at the office. She also learned that everyone had eaten sandwiches and was in their respective rooms. Mia instructed him to wash his face and go to his room.

"Hey Buddy, you don't want to get permanent caramel streaks on those chocolate-colored cheeks, do you?" That was their inside joke which was rewarded with a "No" and a half-hearted chuckle.

"You're not going away to any juvenile delinquent center. You're going to be fine. I'm on my way." Mia then plugged her phone into the charger and began the four-hour drive back home.

Since it was after hours, Mia couldn't reach her mom at the office. She tried to call her mom's cell, but it just rang. As she was driving, she asked God for an answer to Jamari's problems. She prayed for the knowledge, strength, and wisdom to handle this seemingly impossible situation. Mia also said a prayer for their father who was out of the country on assignment. He'd been gone for almost two months and she prayed that his tour would be over soon.

Three hours and thirty minutes later, she finally pulled over to refuel and take a break. Mia was never a drinker or a smoker, and tonight, she was especially grateful for the abstinence. Everyone was toasting and celebrating and the entire firm got to see the looser sides of the otherwise well-tailored Legal Staff.

While perusing the service station, she chuckled remembering her colleague, Richard, with all inhibitions removed. His renditions and gyrations while singing along to "YMCA" had Mia cracking up in the aisle. Because she knew that she was thirty minutes away from ground zero, she allowed herself this laugh — and did she ever. By the time she got to the register, she was wiping tears and barely able to stand up.

Mia was pleased to see the short, blond attendant grinning from ear to ear after bearing witness to her laughing episode in the candy aisle. He asked what had gotten her so tickled, and as Mia attempted to share, she remembered Danielle swinging her sparkly red cardigan in circles above her head while dancing to "Girls Just Wanna Have Fun."

At that point, she completely lost her composure bursting into more sniggering and tears. Her sides were literally cramping, and she was thankful for hitting the ladies' room moments earlier as she would have definitely peed herself. Mia straightened her torso to fend off the second wave of giggle-induced cramping and finally stammered, "I'd also like to get twenty dollars on pump one."

At this point, the middle-aged attendant was in stitches laughing at Mia. That contagious laugh was… well…contagious. Mia was still wiping tears as she removed the nozzle and began pumping her gas. The attendant came out to check the garbage. Experience told Mia that the garbage was the last thing he was checking out. It was especially obvious as the containers were all but empty.

She recalled how puffy the waste bag in the can next to the store front was — a clear indication that the trash had been recently changed. Remembering the task at hand, Mia cordially offered, "That certainly makes up for missing Thursday's workout. All we need is to have one laugh like that at least once every other day and we can skip the gym."

A few seconds later, Mia bid a wonderful evening to the still hopeful attendant and unlocked her gold 1999 Honda Accord LX — her first major purchase as a gainfully-employed adult. Mia remembered taking three days to learn to drive her new car as it was a manual and she'd only driven a manual gear shift once before. The salesman offered Mia a deal she couldn't refuse. She smiled thinking about her father's incredulous expression when she'd called him to help drive her new car off the lot. Ever since then, Mia and "Goldie" were inseparable. Goldie was her baby and she was thankful for it.

Suddenly, it was back. That weird feeling that someone was watching. Mia surveyed her surroundings. Other than a lonesome owl and the occasional swooshes of rubber speeding across pavement in the distance, the night was silent. The only vehicles in the lot were Goldie and the attendee's green Toyota. Even still, she sensed eyes and not just those of the enamored man who she'd just met. The sense was almost palpable. She quickly hopped into her trusty transport locking the doors and speeding off.

Mia couldn't put her finger on that eeriness. It wasn't regular, but she'd sometimes feel it while jogging the bike paths and occasionally when at the mall. Once, she'd felt eyes while walking out of court and swore someone had been eyeing her as she brought in her groceries. But Mia never saw anyone — never noticed anyone lurking – ever. Even still, she knew she wasn't imagining things. There was something to it.

She surveyed the highway intently for several miles looking for any headlights that mimicked her path. After 20 minutes, Mia blasted the radio and sang along at the top of her lungs – eventually quelling her fears. With her sense of security almost completely restored, she reminded herself that she was safe in God's hands. The karaoke-infused mileage allayed her fears allowing her to refocus and prepare for battle.

It was 11:45 p.m. when Mia turned into the driveway of her family's two-story white-bricked Victorian. Mia came home at least once every other month, but the view of the house as she ascended the spruce tree-lined driveway was always spectacular. Multi-colored hydrangeas and peach and red rose bushes hugged the lower porch while ivy inched up the trellis. Path lighting softly illuminated the sidewalk and driveway. There was a crème cherub fountain in the center of the yard that always prompted conversation and the spontaneity of quarter tossing. Mia fondly remembered the many ice cream sundaes funded by that wonderful water display.

Her parents' home was warm and welcoming. But that was just it...it was no longer her parent's home. Mia's parents had been together for twenty-eight years. Her mom found out that she was pregnant with Mia well before they'd planned to have children. As a result, their wedding plans were moved up by a couple of years – yes, years. From then on, Elaine and Ramon had been the perfect couple, or so everyone thought.

When Ramon announced that he was leaving right after Mia completed her freshman year in college, everyone was shocked – everyone except her mom. Later, Elaine revealed that she'd known for years that Ramon was unhappy being home. He never ran around or cheated. The highly esteemed photojournalist just had an incurable thirst for adventure. Despite his adoration for his family and a successful career, he longed for the exotic, foreign assignments that were largely unattainable as a married, family man.

After sticking with the marriage and staying at home for over two decades, he could no longer stand it. Ramon just felt like a piece of him was missing. He and Elaine had had plans and dreams, all of which became largely moot after Elaine's unexpected pregnancy. They were supposed to see the world with him capturing every moment until they were ready to settle down. Sure, they kept a few promises to travel. Together, they'd been to Mount Rushmore, Cape Cod, and Cancun, and even Africa. As fun as visiting and photographing these marvelous places was, Ramon longed for more – for meaning.

Elaine swore that she would divorce him if he decided to travel into dangerous territory "just to take pictures," as she crassly put it. As difficult as it was to leave his family, Ramon equated staying with dying a slow, painful death. He knew that he would always be there financially for his children and that Elaine was a great mom. So, the day Mia came home after also concluding her stint as an At-Risk youth counselor, Ramon barbecued his famous ribs and served them with a side of homemade potato salad, greens, deviled eggs, and macaroni and cheese.

Mia assumed that the meal was in celebration of her wrapping up the year successfully and moving on to bigger and better things. She'd been wrong. Ramon sat the family down and told everyone that he'd taken a job as an imbedded photographer with the Special Forces and would be leaving the country. Initially, he'd been bombarded with inquiries about the location and subjects of photographs, etc. Shortly after all the questioning began, Mia noticed a forlorn spirit from her father and a terseness emanating from her mother.

Two days later, Elaine made good on her promise and filed for divorce. The following weeks were extremely brusque in the Copeland home and were ultimately the beginning of Jamari's troubles.

MIA CUT THE engine and took a deep breath. Pulling back the cover of her sunroof, she stared up into the night sky. Searching the floating stars of the heavens, she sighed. "Father, in the name of Jesus, thank You for allowing me to make it here safely and please guide everyone that is still traveling. Let them make it to their destinations safely. Lord, please give Mom, Jamari, and me the strength to endure this test. Give us wisdom and insight and help us come up with a resolution. Lord, You know Mari's a good boy. Please show us what to do. In Jesus name, Amen."

Mia opened her car door, pulled her strappy two and a half inch black pumps back on, and hurried up the steps.

CHAPTER 3:
In a Word – BATTLE

*M*IA PAUSED AT the family's elegant etched glass front door. She was always amazed at how merely inserting her key and turning the knob brought back such a sense of nostalgia. She reminisced back to the day they moved in. She'd been an energetic four-year-old happily riding her tricycle around the arched driveway as her extended family hustled in and out of the house offloading furnishings, suitcases, and lamps.

She still remembered the demure yellow spaghetti sundress sprinkled with tiny pink and white flowers. Her clear jelly sandals revealing pink toenail polish as her tiny feet pushed the white petals a million miles an hour. Mia remembered how her twin ponytails flapped almost in unison with the folds of her dress.

Nothing was removing her smile that day. Not even the scrapes from falling off her trike twice. She was on top of the world. Mia fondly remembered running up and down the halls, dodging family members while blissfully flipping the light switches on and off in each room as she passed, stopping briefly to make carpet angels in the floor of every empty room. That had been one of the happiest days of her life.

She was excited about moving into such a large home. After all, until that moment, the threesome lived in a cramped one-bedroom studio apartment. Ramon & Elaine lived there for two years before Elaine became pregnant. It was cheap and they were able to amass a respectable savings. The pair decided to stay there after Mia was born and continue saving their money. It was the six years of savings that allowed the young couple the ability to afford their dream home.

Years later, their beautiful abode wasn't the same source of joy or security that it had been the day they'd moved in. It was no longer the keeper of the family joys that came with the arrival of each new sibling. Now, it just felt like a place where they just lived.

Back to reality… "Ok, Lord. You go before me." With that, she turned the knob and pushed open the front door.

The first thing that hit Mia upon entry was the smell of baked fish, okra, and fried white potatoes with onions. "Good Lawd. We're gonna have to discuss this in the kitchen," Mia said to herself. After all, she'd only stopped once during the four-hour drive and that was for gas and gum. Prior to that, Mia had only eaten hors d'oeuvres at the celebration. "Focus, girl," she said scolding herself and her stomach. There were much more important issues at hand.

She kicked off the snakeskin heels, hung her cute black clutch on the coat rack, and placed her keys on foyer's counter. Just as she turned the corner. . . "The next time you get on the road without calling me first, I'mma whoop you." It was Elaine walking towards her from the living room.

"Hey Momma," smiled Mia. They shared an extraordinary Mother-Daughter bond – one that really began blossoming when Mia contracted Malaria at age three while they vacationed in Port-au-Prince, Haiti. Up until that time, Elaine hadn't been the most adoring or attentive mom to Mia. Truth be told, she'd come along years before Elaine had ever thought of having children. At the time of Mia's birth, she hadn't been remotely ready to be a mom; however, when faced with the prospect of losing her beautiful baby, Elaine snapped into full "Mommy Mode" – moving heaven and earth for Mia – and it had been that way ever since.

So, when Elaine threatened to get Mia, she knew her mother was just speaking out of worry. "I did try to call you, but you didn't pick up; your cell phone just rang." They kissed each other on the cheek then hugged for what seemed like an hour.

When they broke the embrace, Mia saw tears streaming from her mother's eyes. Her heart plummeted. In all her years, Mia had never seen her mother cry – even through the divorce and watching Ramon, the love of her life, her husband, and father of her children, walk away. She bear-hugged Elaine and tenderly walked her back into the living room.

Mia knew that whatever Jamari did this time was on a whole different level. After grabbing tissue from the lacquer burgundy coffee table and dabbing Elaine's eyes, Mia grabbed Elaine's hands and asked what Jamari did.

Elaine told her that while cleaning the cupboards four days ago, she'd found $25,000 in a flour container. It had been sitting empty in the cabinet for probably a year and she'd never touched it. Truth be told, it had been there so long that it almost faded into the background. She finally decided to get rid of the canister since it was just taking up space. Elaine added that when she picked it up, a box of crackers which had been in front of the canister fell forward. While attempting to catch the box, she ended up dropping the container. On impact, the top came open and out popped a large plastic Ziploc bag.

"I almost passed out, Amia. I tried to think of all the possible reasons for that money to have been in that flour container. Then I remembered your dad saying when he left that he'd tucked away some money for us in the house." She sniffed and dabbed tears. "I was too pissed at Ramon at the time to even acknowledge him or ask where it was, so I called him. He said that the money was in the fireproof safe that he'd built into the garage." Elaine smiled and shook her head.

"We've lived here twenty-two years. I never questioned his insistence on building out the garage and hanging that snaggle-toothed picture of you in that ugly purple striped turtleneck smack dab in that corner." Mia smiled.

Elaine shook her head and continued. "Ramon asked me who'd been at the house. There hasn't been anyone other than the kids. Your dad then suggested that I move the box, put it in the safe, and watch. I think he knew that it belonged to Mari." Elaine continued through tears. "Two days later, I heard Shamir screaming, 'I don't know what you're talking about. What can?'"

Mia's jaw dropped. "Mom, please tell me that he's not dealing drugs."

Elaine didn't answer her oldest daughter. Instead, another tear fell as she recounted how Jamari went into Jordyn and Bria's room screaming at them and demanding to know who had touched the can of flour. "I ran upstairs pretending not to know anything and asked him what the problem was. He said that one of the kids took the flour can and that he needed it for a science project."

"I couldn't believe it. That money was Jamari's. I then told him that I could empty the sugar container and he could use that." Then a look that Mia had never seen before came across Elaine's face. It was fear. "Mia, you should have seen the rage in that boy's eyes when he pushed past me. I almost fell down the stairs. Mari looked in every closet and trash can. He ran outside and checked the shed and outside trash can, then came back in screaming about that container."

Elaine recounted how he'd all but tore up the

kitchen cabinets when Elaine got back to the kitchen followed by her three youngest children. When Jamari started to panic, Elaine sent the kids upstairs and spoke to him alone. She recalled his nervousness and frantic searching of the refrigerator, oven, and microwave. After demanding that he tell her what was going on and asking why he needed that container and he couldn't use another one, Jamari confessed that he'd put some money in the container.

"I asked him how much money and where he'd gotten money from, but he didn't answer. He just kept looking. I told him that I would take my belt off if he didn't answer me. That is when he told me that he was holding some money for a guy he knew. I asked him what guy and how much money. Mia, panic came across his face again and he told me $25,000. Then I asked whose money it was. Mia, a tear fell from his eye and he looked like he was going to shit his pants. He told me that the guy sells drugs and that he asked him to hold the money until Friday because police were checking him out."

"I finally got Mari to go to bed after convincing him that we'd find it. Your dad didn't believe a word of it and told me to check his room when he went to school." Elaine looked heartbroken as she recalled returning to the house this morning after dropping the kids off at school. She'd dressed as though she was heading to work, so the kids would not be suspicious and for whatever reason, Elaine decided to park her white Lexus in the garage, which she never did.

After searching Mari's room for ten minutes, she

found a shoebox in the back of his closet containing marijuana, white rocks, and phone numbers. Horrified and in sheer disbelief of Jamari's audacity, Elaine immediately emptied the box and retrieved the flour container from the safe. Elaine's next move was to grab a baseball bat, then she waited for Jamari to return from school.

By two thirty that afternoon, Elaine had spoken to Ramon three times and she'd contacted Jamari's Parole Officer. He'd previously been in trouble for skipping school and stealing a diamond watch from a department store as well as chips and some granola bars from the local convenience store. Elaine left a message for their attorney who'd just saved Jamari from a year in Juvenile Detention.

Normally, Elaine would have picked up Bria, Jordyn, and Shamir, but that day she'd arranged for her best friend since middle school, Kerry, to pick the youngsters up.

"I'm telling you Kerry, I know what I'm doing. My gut tells me I'm right and you know I always trust my instincts," said Elaine.

"Elaine, are you sure you don't want me to come over too? On second thought, I'll send David and William. You don't need to confront him while no one's there."

"No, Kerry. He's my son. I brought his happy behind into this world and I will damn sure take his dumb dope-dealing ass out if he even blinks at me wrong," Elaine retorted to her bestie.

"Mia, not long after I hung up with Kerry waiting on Mari's ignorant ass to come home, a red E-Class pulled into the driveway."

"Since Mari didn't think I'd be home for another hour with the kids, he invited the driver in." Elaine snorted and continued, "Now, number one, that boy knows that he's supposed to be walking home and number two, absolutely no one is allowed in this house when I'm not home." Elaine ran her tongue across her teeth and pursed her lips.

"I just leaned up against the counter and waited on them to come in. I stayed in the kitchen because that's the first place Mari goes when he comes home and sure enough...his simple ass came pimping around that corner and...Lord have mercy, Mia, I swung that bat so hard that I busted the damn refrigerator. Knocked the door clean off the hinges."

By this time, the hot flashes of menopause combined with her boiling blood forced Elaine to strip down to her orange and white shell tank top. She began pacing and fanning herself while dabbing her face and neck with the tissues.

"Oooh, I thank God I didn't hit him 'cause you'd be visiting me down at the County." Elaine paused for a while, then continued, "But you know what? I was so outdone with that little Negro that I swung the bat again. That's how the pantry door got split. Child, I would have killed that boy, if I hadn't used all my energy on the first two swings."

Mia cracked a smile for the first time since hugging her mom.

Elaine gave her the "I ain't joking" look, pursed her lips, rolled her eyes, and looked back at Mia grinning. "The next thing I knew, wheels were burning rubber out of the driveway. I looked outside and found Jamari hiding in a corner of the porch. I made him come back into the house and sit at the table where I had placed the shoe box."

"He just dropped his head and said that it wasn't his." Elaine tilted her head towards the breakfast nook. "You see that the table is missing, right?"

Between the fish in the air and Elaine's shocking tears, Mia hadn't even noticed. Her interest piqued; she stood and leaned towards the breakfast nook, which previously boasted a large oval table with 8 chairs. "Okayyyyyy. I'm not gonna ask what happened to the table. All I want to know is if he finally admitted it."

"Of course, he did. Shit, he knew that if that refrigerator, pantry door, and oak table didn't put a dent in this titanium bat, that his narrow ass didn't stand a chance."

By now, Elaine's fiery Jamaican accent was on full display. Normally, you'd never know that Elaine's parents moved from the Island to the states when she was eight. Now in her 50s, the accent only showed up when she was a week-and-a-half past pissed.

"Mia, I let him know that he had one opportunity to tell the truth and then I would start swinging." Elaine recalled Jamari's whole story of having to borrow lunch money five months ago because he'd forgotten his. The boy who lent it had a brother who was a well-known drug dealer.

"Since Mari borrowed the money, he had to pay him back by doing a 'run.' After the first run, came another run and another. He just kept doing runs. Long story short, $20,000 of the $25,000 belonged to the dealer, who by the way was the one who dropped him off here, and the other $5000 was Mari's to keep. The weed and rocks were Mari's. He was selling them. The phone numbers were his customers'. He even showed me his cell phone. When the hell did this boy get a cell phone?"

Elaine was up again pacing while simultaneously fanning the internal flames. "That explains why he was suddenly so damn popular. Everyone came by to 'play video games in his room.' They'd stay for about 15 minutes and be gone, and it has been like that for months now."

"Mari's grades have slipped. Not to mention that while I was searching his room, I found all kinds of jewelry and new sneakers under his bed. I guess he's been financing all these purchases with this 'part-time gig' of his."

Mia dropped her head backwards and shook it in disbelief. She was heartbroken and stunned that they were talking about her brother, the tall, lanky cutie pie track star with the mad basketball skills. After taking another deep breath, she asked Elaine where Jamari was.

"Upstairs. He should be packing because his ass

is leaving on Friday. I'm sorry, Amia, but I won't have it. Not in my house. I've got impressionable little ones who at this point are all afraid of that boy. He won't listen. He's just hard to deal with. I know he's upset about Ramon leaving and the divorce. Hell, everyone's upset. But it's been three years. We're all still dealing with it, but something's gotta give. And since this is my house..." Elaine stopped pacing, dabbed her drenched forehead and declared through clenched teeth, "He's the something."

"Mom let me talk to Jamari before you make this final. He messed up...big time, I don't dispute or condone any of it. But let me talk to him, please. Before you do anything, please, Mom," Mia begged.

"Mia, I've made up my mind, but go on up there. I'm sure he's awake."

Before knocking on Mari's door, Mia looked in on her little sisters, Jordyn and Bria. They were both knocked out. Bria, the older of her two little sisters, and an incredibly wild sleeper, had her legs and arms strewn everywhere. Mia wondered how she made it through the night without falling out of her brass twin bed. She noted that Bria would need a bigger one soon. After all, she was eight and as wild as she slept, that poor bed was probably begging for mercy.

Bria reminded Mia so much of herself at that age. Very friendly and a consummate peacekeeper. She'd do anything to make everyone happy. Mia smiled to herself as she shifted Bria closer to the back side of her bed and kissed her sister's forehead. She then tiptoed over to her youngest sister, Jordyn's, bed.

Being born two months premature left Jordyn very petite. Though seven and a half, her stature was that of a four or five-year-old. Mia kissed her baby sister's forehead and shook her head while reflecting on her conversation with Elaine last week about the dainty, firecracker. She'd been named after their favorite athlete because, while dangerously preemie, they knew that this baby girl would find a way to win – just as her namesake had always done.

Yes, she was petite, but there was hell to pay for anyone who dared mess with her. "Tiny but deadly," Mia whispered, shook her head, and grinned. The pint-sized, redheaded baby of the Copeland family definitely inherited all of Elaine's temperaments.

After leaving the girl's door cracked, Mia walked down the hall to her little brother, Shamir's, room. At nine years old, Shamir was the third oldest of the kids behind Mia and Mari. His television was still on silhouetting all the sports paraphernalia adorning his room. This kid was hands down, the ultimate sports fanatic. From football to tennis, he played them – and knew the stars of each sport. She swore that Shamir would go to school on a full athletic scholarship and ultimately go into sports broadcasting. As she got closer to his bed, Mia changed her mind. "Boy, as handsome as you are, you'd better be in pictures."

"Oooh wee, Mom, you're gonna have trouble with the girls from this one," Mia mused. Shamir was tall and dark, just like their dad. His waves so defined that a surfer could seriously hang ten. Combine that hair, thick eyebrows, and killer smile with an honor student who is also a jock and you have the ultimate chick magnet. "Swee-pee, I'm glad you still think girls have cooties." Mia shook her head and kissed Shamir's cheek. Then, she left his room and started around the corner to Mari's room.

CHAPTER 4:
In a Word– PURPOSE

"*M*ARI?" MIA WHISPERED while tapping on his door and simultaneously opening it. She heard his television and flipped the light switch. Mari was sitting on his bed with his knees drawn up to his chest. Mia stretched out her arms as Mari climbed off the bed and all but collapsed in her arms. As embarrassed as he was about messing up, Mari knew that Mia would always be his safe place to land. No matter what he did, Mia always had his back.

"I'm sorry, Mia. I'm so sorry," he said almost inaudibly.

"Mari, what were you thinking? Dealing drugs? $25,000? Here at our house?" Mia searched Mari's eyes for answers while firing off questions.

Almost inaudibly, Mari explained that he missed his dad and that he didn't feel like he fit in at home. Shamir, Bria, and Jordyn were all around the same age. They all played with each other. Mari was older and wasn't interested in playing their games. "Mom always wants me to babysit. I can't run track or play basketball this year because no one is home to be with them," he mumbled and flung his arms towards the hallway referencing his sleeping siblings.

Mia detected resentment in his voice. After all, he was thirteen. He wanted to be a normal kid. Her thoughts were interrupted when Mari started explaining that he always took care of the kids. He made snacks when they got home. He helped with homework and started dinner every day.

"Mia," Mari began bawling as though he'd lost in triple overtime by a buzzer beater. "I'm not their dad. Ramon Copeland is. He's supposed to be here. It ain't fair. I'm a kid, Mia," he sobbed.

"I just want to be a kid."

"Mari, I hear you, but what if Shamir decided to sell drugs because he was angry about something? What if he told you he wanted to do it? What would you say? Better yet, what *could* you say to him, Jamari?"

"I'd tell him not to do it. I don't knooooow, Mia. I don't wanna think about Shamir doing that."

"Why not? If you – his big brother – can do it, why can't he?"

"Or better yet, what if Jordyn and Bria played hide-and-seek and decided to hide in your closet or under your bed?" Then grabbing her brother firmly and while resisting competing urges to hug and shake him, she continued.

"Look at me, Mari. Look at me," she commanded. "Did you ever think about what would have happened if your sisters had eaten those rocks thinking they were candy? Did you?"

"Noooooo, Mia. Stop please," he begged. "I'm sorry, OK?"

"Sweetheart, sorry can't fix everything. I love you. You know that. But I need you to know that sorry wouldn't bring either one of them back. Would you really want to spend the rest of your life knowing that the drugs you were selling killed one of your sisters?"

By this time, the gravity of months of nonchalance and insolence hit Mari full speed. The formerly steel-faced thirteen-year old was remorsefully weeping in his sister's arms. And while he'd received lectures from teachers, principals, his parents, attorneys and parole officer, no one had ever been able to reach Mari the way Mia could.

A few minutes passed before Mari succeeded in regaining his composure. He paused a second more before continuing.

"I didn't want to sell drugs, Mia. I didn't need the money. I was doing it because Mom needed me to help her out all the time. I thought that money would help, and I wouldn't have had to stay at home all the time because Mom would have been able to stay home with them.

"I knew Mom wouldn't take the money from me, so I'd always put an extra $20 in her wallet or in the glove compartment or in clothes that she didn't wear all the time or any other place like the junk drawer or something like that. That way, it looked like she was always just finding money."

At that moment, Mia remembered multiple conversations over the past few months wherein Elaine mentioned finding money in the house. She even joked that the house was being haunted by a forgetful millionaire because she kept finding money in the most random places.

Mia was speechless. Mari was trying to fill Dad's role as provider so Mom didn't have to work so hard.

"I hear you, buddy. I really do, but you realize now that this can't ever be the answer, right? This solves nothing."

Mari nodded and then . . .

"Mia, can you ask Dad to come back home?"

This simple, but profound question completely shattered her heart. A full five seconds passed before the words finally escaped her constricted throat and past her lips.

"Oh Buddy. I know you miss Dad. I miss him too. He'll be home someday soon," she managed.

Mia scolded herself for not recognizing the level of desolation Mari had been shouldering since Ramon's departure. While Mia missed her dad's regular presence and their impromptu breakfast dates, she could busy herself with legal statutes. When the anguish of her parents' divorce threatened to overtake her, she'd find solace through volunteerism. She realized that her little brother didn't have the benefit of any constructive distractions.

Almost entirely emotionally spent, Mia tapped into her constant source of strength. Cradling Jamari's head, she just began praying, "Father, in the name of Jesus, it's me again. I'm coming to you tonight lifting up my brother, Mari. Lord, please ease his heart, ease his mind. God, wrap your arms around him and release your peace upon him. God, he is your son and he's been having a hard time. Lord, I know that You can do all things. Help him Lord. Guide him in the right ways. Shield Mari from this pain. Please God. In Jesus name, Amen."

A few moments later, she instructed Mari to wash his face so that he could get in bed. Mia lay next to him and sang him to sleep — something that she hadn't done since he'd jumped out of their 100-year-old oak tree while in Kindergarten and came home sporting a full arm cast signed by an Emergency Room physician and two attending nurses.

Mia walked into Elaine's room. She knew she was in there because she'd heard Elaine ascending the stairs while she was conversing with Jamari. Three years later, it was still weird walking into their bedroom and not seeing her father. Elaine was in bed, TV on, and paging through a Good Housekeeping Magazine.

"Mom?" Mia hiked the silk dress slightly and scooted onto the edge of the king bed. "Mari was selling drugs so that he could give the money to you."

Elaine rolled her eyes in disbelief.

"No, really, Mom. The 'Sugar Daddy Ghost?' That was Mari ensuring that you always had money on you. He thought that if he made enough money that you could stay at home with the kids and he could be a kid again."

"I don't believe that crap for a minute. That boy is just out of control. He can tell you that because you're not here. He figures you'll believe him.

"I've been through too much with him. Your father is God knows where. Sudan? Jordan? Niger? I can't keep up. He's somewhere out of the country and I can't send Mari to him. I love Mari, but I no longer have the strength to deal with it." She paused, then continued, "I hope you didn't think you would change my mind. I already told you, he's out of here come Friday." Elaine had literally had enough and without question, Mari's stint at the Copeland home had officially ended.

"No, I'm not gonna try to change your mind." Mia winked and smiled at Elaine. "That would be a waste of time anyway. I'll need those breaths later on in life."

Elaine smiled back at her eldest daughter, her and Ramon's oldest source of pride.

"I'm taking Mari back with me tomorrow."

Elaine immediately began shaking her head. "No. No, Mia, you're not. You've got a life. You've got a great job, great career, and that's what you need to focus on. Mari's thug-life wanna be ass will be fine. He was man enough to make this bed, let him be man enough to sleep in it."

"Mom," Mia retorted, "Mari's not a man. He's a thirteen-year-old who is helping you raise three children. He's angry because he can't be a kid. The divorce isn't anyone's fault, but Mari has been kinda thrown into an adult's role. He's a teenager, Mom. He just wants to be a kid and do kid things."

"What do you want me to do, Mia? I'm doing the best I can. We all have to sacrifice." She stopped and thought about it. "All those kids out there whose parents have divorced. You don't see them slinging drugs or being blatantly disrespectful, do you? The answer is no, Amia. You are not taking Mari with you."

"Mom, I love and respect you. You know that."

Mia swallowed while conjuring up her most exemplary courtroom etiquette to eloquently state and hold her position with her mother. She took a deep breath and continued cautiously (after all, Mia had been on the receiving end of a few of Elaine's best whoopings and still held her mother's power in high regard).

"Mom, you and Dad always told us that if we saw a stray that we should feed it and then tell someone who could help. You also said that if we saw someone who needed help, we should do our best to help, even if it meant that we had to give up something that we wanted."

"Oh no, Mia..."

"Mom," Mia insisted, "I remember when I was about

nine years old, we went out to eat at Sally's on Western Ave. We saw that single mom with her kids digging in her purse counting up her change to feed everyone. You and Dad looked at each other and then ended up paying for their dinner. You also gave her gas money and the three of us went back home to eat sandwiches because we didn't have enough money left over for us to eat at Sally's too. Remember that?"

"Yes, Mia...but this is diff..."

Mia cut her off and held her hand out of respect. "Mom, Mari is the stray and I'm going to take him. You're that mom and I'm going to help you, too. Will it be a sacrifice? Yes, it will. But I know my brother. He's still that beautiful boy that you gave birth to. He's the same boy who buried the pigeon in the woods under the maple tree so that it wouldn't get too hot from the sun's rays. Remember that, Mom?"

Mia smiled and continued, "Remember when he took responsibility for breaking your watch when it was really Dad who'd stepped on it?" They both laughed and Elaine acknowledged that he was willing to go down in flames just so she wouldn't yell at Ramon.

"Mari's a little off course, Mom. We...you and I, can help him get back on track. I love him, Mom, and so do you. Juvenile Detention isn't for Jamari Copeland. He's not a delinquent. You know it and I know it." Mia spoke from her heart and innermost soul. Her argument was that of desperation. After all, this particular defendant was looking at life with a very slim possibility of parole. "Mom, please let me take him. I can help. I know it."

"Mia, I know you want to help, but you don't need him cutting up on you. What if he gets down there and tries the same thing? You are his sister, not his mother. Why should he listen to you if he wouldn't listen and act right here?"

"Because I'm his last resort. That's why he won't do it again. That's why he'll straighten up. Because I love him too. That's why. Mom, it's just me at my townhouse. I don't have any responsibilities outside of work. I have all the time in the world to spend with him. He can run track and play basketball without worries. You already know I'll make him keep his grades up. Please, Mom. He's only thirteen. He's got too much to offer. Please don't send him away. Let me try."

"Your father is calling again in the morning. We'll talk more about it then. You already know what he's going to say...exactly what I just said."

"Thank you, Mom."

"Don't be thanking me."

"I know but thank you for listening. We can make this work. I know it."

After warming up a dinner plate, Mia and Elaine spent another hour talking about her dress, life in Pittsburgh, work, and the highly publicized trial that her firm had just won.

MUFFLED SOUNDS FROM the patio woke Mia from her slumber. She had cracked her windows before turning in to allow the air to fully circulate throughout her room. Mia stepped over to the window and was able to hear Elaine on the phone with her father. She heard Elaine respond to Ramon. "Uh huh, that's what I told her. Mari just needs to take his punishment. Mia is just beginning her life. She doesn't need to be worried about that boy."

Mia's heart sank. Just then, she heard Elaine say, "Alright then, I'll tell her in the morning..."

Before she knew it, Mia had scrambled across the bed, grabbed the cordless phone, and chimed in. "Daddy, please listen to me."

"Mia!" Elaine shouted.

"Hey baby," Ramon replied with the tone of a professor counseling an underachieving student. "Mia, it's not your responsibility. It's not right for us to allow him to uproot life, as you know it. We've tried it all, counseling, punishment, even rewards for good behavior. What if he doesn't straighten up? What if you get fired because of his antics?" He paused, then continued, "No, Mia. I can't let you do it."

By this time, Mia had flown down the stairway's thirteen steps seemingly without having touched any and joined Elaine outside on the patio. She was barefoot and oblivious to the cool early Spring morning air. Mia's eyes locked with Elaine's attempting to pierce her soul. She was begging them both not to send Jamari off. "I'm twenty-six. I understand that I'm still young, but I'm an adult. I'm the responsible adult that you raised and prepared me to be. I can reach him, I know it.

"I don't like it," countered Elaine. "What about the long hours you put in at work? Where is Jamari going to be then?"

Fortunately, Mia had already thought out the game plan during her four-hour drive up to her parent's home. Jamari would go to practice right after school. Mia would pick Mari up and swing by her house for dinner. If she had to go back to the office, she'd take Mari with her. After all, it was a law firm. He had plenty of books to read and space to do his homework. She'd also decided what chores he'd be responsible for and when he would do them.

Mia already knew what school Mari would attend and because WW&M was so well known, she was sure that she could get leniency from the judge regarding the terms of his parole. She explained all of this and more to her parents who both eventually conceded.

"Ok, ok, counselor in training." chuckled Ramon. "Mia, It's obvious that you've given this great thought and think you know what you're doing...Mari can go with you. It can't be tomorrow, because we have to get him withdrawn and talk to the judge, his attorney, and Parole Officer."

After hearing "Parole Officer," Elaine looked directly at her oldest daughter and said, "I know you love the Lord, but Jamari ain't no angel."

Mia smiled and answered, "I know, Momma, but none of us are. Some of us have obvious flaws that can be fixed with just a little help. Others have issues that will only be known once they've driven themselves senile trying to conceal them."

Whilst that statement applied wholeheartedly to the current situation, Amia meant that more broadly. She was speaking also to Ramon and Elaine's current marital situation and to an unspoken uneasiness that showed up occasionally. There were certain times of the year that were terser than others and she never quite understood why.

"And the Church said: 'Amen.'" added Ramon playfully. "But for real, Mia, if Mari so much as leaves his socks on the floor, I'm leaving Australia and...well, I'll just leave it at that."

"Ok, Daddy."

"Alright, baby girl, get some sleep. You're about to climb Everest and need your rest."

"Ok, Daddy. I love you and miss you."

"I love you too, Mia and I am so proud of you."

Elaine commented on Mia's persistence and tenacity, to which Ramon chuckled and agreed. "She got that from her momma."

That was one thing that Mia admired. No matter

what happened between the two of them, Elaine and Ramon were on the same team when it came to the kids and nothing was gonna change that. They'd never argue with the kids around and would even end phone conversations on a civil, surprisingly friendly note.

After hanging up, Mia and Elaine hugged for a couple minutes. Elaine reminded her that she didn't have to do this. She also told Mia that she did not have to feel like she was stuck with Mari if he started acting out.

"I know Mom. I'll be fine."

With the weight of the world partially lifted from her shoulders, Mia finally noticed that she could see both her and Elaine's breath and that she'd been in such a hurry to get downstairs that she was only wearing an oversized T-shirt and her favorite tattered linen high school PJs.

"Good Lord, Mate. It's a bit chilly," Elaine remarked in her best Australian accent.

"All right, Mum, and it's 4:30," copied Mia. "Time to hit the hay."

CHAPTER 5:
In a Word – RESCUE

*T*HE SCENT OF bacon, buttermilk pancakes, and fresh coffee wafted into Mia's old bedroom through the air vents. As she woke, Mia noticed little shadows under her door. She tiptoed to the door avoiding the creaky floorboard at the end of her bed and snatched it wide-open scaring Jordyn and Bria half to death – evident by their shrieks. Mia knew it was them and hugged her sisters tightly. She headed downstairs with one sister tucked under her left arm and the other riding piggyback.

Shamir ran and met the squealing trio as they were descending. Mia put the girls down so that she could hold onto Shamir while blowing raspberries on his cheeks. He screamed and desperately tried to pull away but enjoyed every second. Walking around the corner, Mia saw Elaine sitting on a barstool sipping coffee. She was surprised to find that the source of the morning's delicious aroma was none other than the man of the hour – Jamari Copeland.

He'd made the entire breakfast complete with scrambled cheese eggs, grits, and orange juice.

"Good morning." Mia smiled at her nervous brother while winking at Elaine. "Poor thing," Mia thought to herself, "he doesn't have a clue what was decided last night."

Shamir, Jordyn, and Bria inquired about the missing table, broken fridge, and pantry. Mia told them that Elaine was renovating the kitchen like she had renovated the townhouse. She added that the table was going to be replaced with a newer, cooler one. That was it. No more questions.

The Three Musketeers immediately started cackling about the new kitchen and suggesting new color schemes that ranged from frog boogers green to unicorn pink to sparkly ladybug red. Mia silently congratulated herself. She still had that knack with the kiddos.

Shamir grabbed some milk from Ramon's fridge in the garage. Elaine was thankful for her decision not to get rid of that dingy orange-yellow antique. Fortunately, it cranked right up when Elaine plugged it back in and allowed her to save all of the food in the now busted-up fridge.

After their scrumptious breakfast, Elaine sent the youngest three upstairs to watch cartoons. "Sit down, Mari."

His face and demeanor were all too familiar to Mia. In fact, she'd just seen that look in court yesterday. It was the look of anxious defendants after learning that the jury or judge had reached a verdict.

"Don't think that getting up and making breakfast makes up for anything. I don't care about that. You decided that you don't want to listen to me and even worse, you put this family in danger by dealing drugs. Have you any idea what could have happened to us? Do you care?"

"Mom, I'm..."

"I didn't say you could speak. I called the attorney this morning." Mari's mouth fell open and huge tears began welling.

"Mom, please..."

Elaine's heart ached for her oldest son and his agony, but she remained firm. Her game face intact.

"I still haven't said that you can speak."

Mia held Mari's hand, just as she'd seen Marty, Geoff, and the others do to comfort anxious clients.

Elaine continued, "The attorney will speak with the judge on Tuesday about moving your case to Pittsburgh. Your sister drove all the way out here and had your father and me up for the longest time last night fighting for you." Elaine paused, then continued, "Mari, all Mia has to do is mention that you missed the bus because you woke up late. You will be out of there and at Silver Lakes Detention Center until you're grown. I'm not playing with you either."

Silence filled the kitchen and both women witnessed

an amazing metamorphosis. They watched as his facial expressions moved from desperate, to solemn, to confused, to elated — all within ten seconds. Suddenly, the defiant teen that Elaine had grown to know leaped out of his chair and fell into her lap weeping with thanksgiving. "Don't just thank me. You need to thank your father too."

"Ok Ma. I will. Thank you. Thank you. Thank you." He wept.

"Mom," Mia interrupted, "I'm going to call Marty at the office. I'll just arrange to stay until Wednesday so that we get everything taken care of."

"Uh-uh, Mia. We're not starting that. You will not be missing work for Jamari. You will not get yourself fired behind nonsense. No Ma'am. He'll be fine. You just give me the information and phone numbers. I'll do the rest. Come back on Wednesday. I scheduled the meeting with the attorney for 4:30 p.m."

THE DAYS FOLLOWING Jamari's reprieve were filled with activities. Elaine was busy making after-school care arrangements for the youngest three and meeting with Jamari's attorney.

Jamari was busy packing and playing with his siblings. His biggest task was behaving at all costs. Mia informed her colleagues that her brother would accompany her whenever overtime was required. Mia also prepared the middle school for Jamari's arrival.

The one thing she made sure that she had in place before her brother's move were solid, positive, male role models. Mia ensured that they were available at scheduled intervals to assist her with imparting morals, responsibility, and ownership from a man's perspective. In addition, Mia alerted her Church Family that Mari was coming. After all, it wasn't too long ago that Mia was an active member of her church's youth group.

At twenty-five, she'd graduated from the young adult to the adult side, which was cool but man, the youth programs had it going on. The youth pastors and workers were used to dealing with all types of youth – from abused children, to sexually misguided preteens and youth, to those who've had past histories of violence. They used their life experiences and empathy to guide these youngsters in the way of the Lord. But they never stopped there; the youth workers were famous for their undying nurturing and caring for the kids to ensure their spiritual growth.

MIA LEFT WORK around noon on Wednesday to ensure that she had enough time to meet the attorney and judge for the transfer of guardianship.

Had the secretary not mentioned that Mia should be on the lookout for a midnight blue Jaguar parked alongside of an otherwise unassuming building, Mia would have driven right past the office which turned out to be only two blocks off the Capital Beltway and on the left rather than three blocks and on the right as the secretary had mentioned.

"I hope she tells everyone to look for the Jag. Her directions are terrible. I bet everyone shows up late," she grumbled. After alarming her precious Goldie, Mia headed around the corner where she was met by an impressive, beautifully restored eighteenth-century Colonial.

Though the WW&M office was impeccable and had undeniable character, this office and its commitment to the historic excellence that was the 1820s left her awestruck. Soon, rhythmic clicking tore her stare from the tongue and groove wood floors and three-story wooden columns. It was the secretary and her three-inch navy heels.

"Ms. Copeland?" she asked.

"Yes, but Amia is fine."

"Right this way. Everyone is in the Judge's chamber."

"I'm sure they are. Some great first impression I'm making being the last one here. How is she even working here and giving shoddy directions?" Mia mumbled still irritated.

As usual, she scolded herself, "Focus Amia. Get over it and focus."

She was guided into a chilly wood-paneled room where she found Elaine, Jamari, their attorney, and a court reporter already seated. Moments later, they were joined by Judge Jeffersoni, a short statured Italian woman with a surprisingly friendly demeanor.

Thirty minutes later, Jamari was hers — literally. Everything that he did and everything that happened to him from here on was Mia's responsibility. If he skipped class, it reflected on her.

"Do you understand the terms and conditions that we have discussed and do you furthermore agree to take complete responsibility for the rearing, guidance, healthcare, and well-being of said minor, Jamari Ramon Copeland?"

"Absolutely," Mia answered with the confidence of a billionaire, though the enormity of the proceedings had just hit her. Her steely façade was in staunch opposition with her now queasy stomach. She now regretted her decision to wear the thick beaded necklace as she was sure the ivory spheres were bouncing off of her baby blue blouse with each beat of her racing heart. All Mia knew was that Mari was her brother and there was no way in hell he was going anywhere. Then she reminded herself that that with God all things were possible and that she can do all things through Christ...

Amia's internal pep talk had restored her confidence by the end of the hearing almost matching her convincing exterior. Mia drew strength in knowing that God had never failed her. She was stepping into unchartered territory. She thought about the unknown and the tests to come, but she knew she would succeed. After all, God was in her corner and failure was not an option.

Following a severe scolding and warning by Judge Jeffersoni, Jamari was released to Mia. She stood outside the building with Elaine and Jamari thanking their attorney for his intervention.

"No problem," he replied, then turned to Jamari. The attorney extended his hand to the youngster and informed him that he'd seen several cases where another family member stepped in to help rear a wayward child. Of the cases, only two that he knew of had taken their second chances seriously. He then added that both children had adjusted well and have gone on to productive lives.

Mari then turned to Elaine and promised that he would be the third who'd take this opportunity seriously. He then turned to Mia who now seemed more like his guardian angel than his sister. He truly loved Mia and thanked God that she wouldn't give up on him. "I promise, I'll do right, Amia."

Choking down the huge lump in his throat and

blinking off the crocodile tears that were welling, he simply repeated, "I promise."

Mia squeezed her little brother tightly. She kissed the top of his head and whispered, "I know, Mari. I know you will."

With Mari safely on the road with Mia, Elaine called the police and gave them the license plate of the red Mercedes E-Class that she'd seen in her driveway a few days earlier. She told them that she thought the driver was a drug dealer and was trying to get her son involved in drugs. Two days later, the driver, Rosco, was involved in a shootout with police at the mall after his car was spotted. He managed to grab a woman who foolishly decided to run to her car during the exchange. She'd been hoping to get to her car and escape the danger with her twin toddlers.

Instead, she and her babies had become unwitting hostages in what turned out to be a five-hour standoff. Eventually, the negotiator convinced Rosco let the boys and the mother go. He then pointed the gun at the officers in an attempted 'suicide by cop'. The result wasn't death. According to the news reports, three shots hit Rosco paralyzing him from the chest down and he was in critical condition. If he lived, he'd have to answer for the 30 pounds of marijuana, 100 bags of crack, and a $85,000 cash that was found hidden in makeshift compartments in his car. The good news for Elaine, at least, was that Rosco wouldn't be showing up again any time soon. Still, Ramon encouraged her to get a gun – just in case.

CHAPTER 6:
In a Word – REASSURANCE

"*M*ARI? MARI? WAKE up. We're here." As he stirred, he recognized the familiar skyline of Pittsburgh that was opening before them. The view of the city as they emerged from the Fort Pitt Tunnel never got old. He'd seen it at least three times a year since Mia first entered college at Carnegie Mellon and it was still spectacular.

Before heading home, Mia decided to stop by the grocery store. She'd been so into the music and engrossed in remembrance of the previous days' events that she hadn't noticed Mari's increasingly terse demeanor. She'd been completely oblivious to the fear and panic that had been steadily compounding inside Mari with the passage of every intersection.

"Ok, what's wrong, Jamari?" Mia asked the instant she pulled into the lot and cut Goldie's engine.

"Mia, what if I mess up?"

He paused for a second while nervously wringing his hands.

"I mean, I'm not going to try to mess up, but what if I don't clean up my room or forget to flush the toilet or I lose the remote? I don't know...what if . . . what if you get tired of me or – ."

"Get tired of you? What are you talking about, Mari? Listen Buddy, no one expects you to be perfect. There's no such thing. You're a kid, Mari. I expect you to listen and do what you're supposed to do. I expect you to respect me and everyone who is deserving of respect. I expect you to go to school and get good grades, to play sports, to make good friends, to have fun, and to grow up into the man that we both know you are meant to be. I'm not going to be Mother Hen, Mari." Then covering his fidgety hands with hers, she continued. "I will be here and I will be fair and firm and *we* will be just fine... okay?"

"Okay," he whispered feeling a little more reassured.

"Good. I know you're going to do well. Now, come on."

As they walked up to the market, Mia stopped short. "First rule of being a man...respect and chivalry. Now, get the door, please."

"Yes Ma'am," he enthusiastically replied and ran ahead to hold open the door. Two other women walked in as he was holding the door.

"Thank you very much, young man," said the first.

"You're such a gentleman," complimented the other.

Both comments left Mari beaming. Mia knew that this was the first in a long line of accomplishments and challenges to come for them both. After paying for her items, Mia instructed Mari to carry a few of the bags. He obliged and held the door for her and another female patron.

Mia would give him a day to rest before she began laying down the law. That was decided during the drive home when she found herself fighting off sleep from her whirlwind week of prepping for Mari's arrival.

As she pulled into her newly paved driveway, Mia prayed for strength, knowledge, and wisdom. Lord knows, she was gonna need it.

The siblings looked at each other, opened their respective doors, and stepped out into their new roles and lives.

CHAPTER 7:
In a Word – GUARDIANS

*I*T WAS THE end of April when Mari's second chance at life began. Since then, he had become the poster child for reform. He cleaned his room and helped with the laundry and dishes. He became involved in the youth group at church and had dove into his schoolwork. His marks were good and his teachers were complimentary.

Mia adjusted her workload so that she only stayed late twice a week. Initially, Mari would sit in the Law Library and do his homework. Often, Mia and her fellow co-workers would call on Mari to pull various volumes and archived cases from the library. With each request, Mari's interest in the information encased between the old, heavy leather volumes became more piqued.

One evening, after searching the entire office twice looking for Mari, she found him in Senior Partner Mike Washington's corner office. She started to apologize for what seemed like Mari's intrusion, when she noticed that the atmosphere was actually quite cozy. She suddenly had the distinct feeling that this hadn't been Mari's first visit to Mike's office.

Mike noticed Mia's confusion and beckoned her into his office and closer to his large maple desk. She noticed Mari's handwriting on a few note pads. To Mia's pleasant surprise, she found that Mari and Mike had been reviewing case notes of an upcoming trial. He was letting Mari get a taste of research and review in an effort to see if he was interested in the inner workings of the other side of the judicial system.

Mia couldn't have been happier; her little brother was thriving. Few people understood how he could have gotten into so much trouble back in Lancaster, except Darren Wilford, a coworker of Mia's.

Darren had been with the firm for four years. He arrived shortly after graduating from Temple University's School of Law. He had chosen to study Pre-Law while an undergrad and on a full-football scholarship and at 6'4, 245 pounds, Darren was a formidable presence in the court room.

Interestingly, though ruggedly handsome, Darren didn't entertain intimate solicitations and had not been linked to any woman. With that, for her first few months at the firm, Mia had actually questioned the powerhouse defense attorney's sexual orientation. Not that she'd really been interested in dating him. To Mia, dating a coworker was an absolute no-go. One thing that confused Mia was that she had caught Darren admiring her more than a few times, but he never hinted interest.

Regardless, she had to admit, Darren was undeniably one of the finest specimens of caramel eye-candy she'd seen in Pittsburgh.

It was two months after Jamari's arrival that Darren found out about his interest in making the football team. With his collegiate background and current status as a camp owner, Darren offered to give Mari some pointers. Initially, Mia was hesitant because of her uncertainty with Darren's background, private life, and sexual preferences. She knew that it was none of her business, but she couldn't help it. She didn't want to sign off on anything that could put Jamari in danger.

She took her concerns to Marty. After all, Marty had given her the job and taken her under his wing. She actually regarded Marty as a second father – the father who was there while Ramon was away.

Marty sat on the edge of his desk and looked out on the city of Pittsburgh through his fifth story windows. He revealed that they'd come to know Darren when he was fourteen. He had been one of the firm's most difficult clients to defend. That was all that Marty disclosed to her that afternoon. "Anything else you want to know; you'll have to get from him directly. And obviously you know that his file has been sealed since he was a juvenile at the time."

Marty patted her shoulder and paused. "You know, Mia, I adore you and have always respected you. You have made us all extremely proud by your actions with Jamari. I know he's your brother and you feel a sense of responsibility, but you aren't acting like someone who is obligated to take care of him. You are committed heart and soul to him and there's nothing that any of us would stop at to make sure you both succeed."

Mia smiled, and confided that she sometimes felt like her world would crash in. Things were going so well that she was sure Satan would try to show up in some way. Marty held her hands and they said a brief prayer of covering and bound up her fears. As Mia began to leave, Marty pulled his beige blazer onto his broad lean shoulders. He then added that if he felt Jamari would have been in any trouble by being around Darren, he wouldn't have paid for him to go to Darren's camp this upcoming summer.

Before Mia could protest about Marty paying Mari's camp fees, he put his hand up and called it a charitable donation from the firm. Mia started to tell him that she could have easily paid for the camp herself, but Marty waived his wrist, again looked out the window, and in an upper-class British accent joked, "That will be all."

Mia was dumbfounded. He'd outsmarted her again. At this time, she'd been at the firm for four years and throughout her tenure, she'd grown to recognize and outsmart the unspoken culture. The partners and staff were well-known for playing One-Up, a one-step-ahead-of-the-other game. To keep the game interesting, the one-up had to be significant and a little time had to pass between each interaction. Mia had lost the last two bouts with Marty and was determined not to lose this one too. "Well, what if I..."

"Overruled." He said this time rendering his best

imitation of Judge Carpenter who was best-known for his extreme impatience and unmistakable country twang.

Mia cracked up laughing. "Oooh, you are so wrong for that one." After a minute, she gathered herself and tried again. "Ok, Marty, listen..."

He stretched his long arm with its Rolex-adorned wrist towards the door and pointed. "Leave, now." That was all he said. No accent this time, just a firm grin and glare to match that firmly pointed index finger.

Knowing she'd been defeated, Mia smiled, rolled her eyes, and headed for the door. After opening the door and stepping into the hallway, she said almost inaudibly, "Motion for a continuance."

"Denied."

They both laughed and agreed to talk later.

CHAPTER 8:
In a Word – INEXPLICABLE

AS SHE HEADED for the firm's recently refurbished kitchen, Mia started thinking about Darren and wondering what he'd been accused of that made him so hard to defend. Did they win? Did he testify? What in the world?

Her thoughts were interrupted by Rhonda, the newly hired Research Analyst who'd inquired about the location of the copy paper. While showing her to the supply closet, Mia complimented her beautiful dark complexion and how her skin glowed against her fashionable crimson pencil skirt. She opted to give Rhonda another quick tour of the entire office while getting to know their newest associate. Upon completion of the tour, Mia joked, "There's gonna be a test later. You must get everyone's name *and* nickname correct." Rhonda laughed and assured Mia that she'd be failing that one. They chatted a little more at Rhonda's desk then Mia headed back to the kitchen to heat up her leftovers and ponder again on Darren's prior legal issue.

She really liked the new kitchen. Having been completed just one month prior, the new galley was designed to fit in with the French Provincial style and era of the office. Because their firm was headquartered in a historical building, the historical society had been there every step of the way to ensure the preservation of the integrity of the era. Twenty-three days later, the partners, associates, and staff had been blown away by their new space. Mia noted that there was something empowering about mixing coffee in a masterfully restored kitchen.

In addition, the massive painting of Marty's sprawling Twin Lakes waterfront cabin added that extra crispness to the atmosphere.

The painting included a massive Weeping Willow at the water's edge and second-story window with a soft yellow glow. Mia recalled Marty's story of the painting and how the cabin came to be. The room with the light belonged to Andrew – the sole child of the owners – and his room was always candlelit. Andrew had never smiled or uttered a word in the seven years since his birth. That is until he saw Marty's great-grandfather, then a two-year old fugitive slave, wandering at the water's edge. Andrew had run to his mother, Lady Madeline and said, "Little Boy."

Lord Michael Worthy, the boy's father wanted to have the emaciated toddler returned, but Lady Madeline refused believing that the child was a gift. The story went that Andrew, who likely had a form of autism, would only speak when "Weeboy" was around. That's the name he was given by Andrew and because the child was too young to give his real name, it stuck.

Lady Madeline and Lord Michael came to love Weeboy as their own. He would be the only other child they would have due to their vast differences in age. Through the years, Weeboy learned to read, write and add because Andrew would only do so in Weeboy's presence. He was vital to Andrew's social development. They played together and slept in the same room and were essentially raised as brothers.

When Weeboy was in his early twenties, Lady Madeline became very ill and with Lord Worthy losing his mental capacities, decided to make Weeboy Andrew's caregiver. In order to be officially recognized, Weeboy had been decreed a son by the Worthys and given their last name.

Lady Madeline had also purchased a slave woman who could cook and clean the mansion. Because Andrew would not live anywhere else, they left their wealth, manor and all of its belongings to Weeboy Worthy. He eventually married Ruthie and freed her. They'd raised their children at the cabin and cared for Andrew until his death. Marty's grandfather had been left the cabin in Weeboy's will. He subsequently left the manor to Marty's father and this is where Marty and his siblings were raised. The cabin had been left to Marty ten years ago and he'd been keeping the treasure as a vacation property.

Smiling at the painting, fond memories of tubing on the lake and enjoying martinis on its extended balcony floated into her forefront. Mia sighed. She couldn't wait until the next WW&M getaway and shindig. The partners' wives hosted the highly anticipated event every summer and definitely knew how to throw a party.

The beeping prompted her to remove the meal and since her coffee had been excessively stirred while she recalled the captivating story of Weeboy Manor, Mia set off to find Darren Wilford. It had been almost an hour since he proposed the one-on-one training for Jamari. With Marty's blessing, Mia would say yes. Maybe she'd eventually learn the mystery of Darren's past. For now, it sure was eating at her.

———~———

"KNOCK, KNOCK?" MIA, said while tapping at the heavy oak door leading into a bright 10 x 10 corner office. Darren Wilford's home away from home was definitely a masculine space featuring his love of sports and highlighting his football camp participants. There were also pictures of his two boxer puppies strategically displayed throughout the office. That was another thing that made Mia question Darren's sexual orientation. There was no denying that this man had an eye for interior decor. Most men she knew couldn't organize their food neatly on a plate, let alone design a whole office.

If you hadn't known Darren Wilford, his office definitely provided insight. It told a great story of its distinguished and athletic occupant. He was cultured and smart, all while being fun-loving and bold. His office walls were the perfect shade of taupe meets olive. They were in stark contrast to his bold, ivory-toned leather accent chairs with gold button tufting. The fifth-year attorney's space was tied together by a large oriental rug.

"He likes harmony," thought Mia. This was evidenced by the colors and texture of the rug which smartly merged the walls, square thatched drapes, and wooden picture frames. "A traditional man with great taste who loves tranquility and is bold," concluded Mia. She surmised the last conclusion by the splashes of aqua and yellow throughout his space. And then there's the aroma of the office. Masculine, but with a hint of lavender. "Wow." Mia wished she had the nerve to ask him to help her with...

"Mia?"

"Huh? Oh sorry. I got caught off guard by the, umm... umm...is that a candle?" Mia asked while sniffing the air and thanking God that she'd had an excuse for being thrown off.

Darren smiled and nodded. "Yeah, I just got it

yesterday. Remember my client who sued her company for firing her two years ago because she took leave to take care of her mom?"

"Yeah."

"She took some of the settlement money and started a candle shop. Smells pretty good, huh?" He asked handing Mia the candle so she could get a full whiff. "Addie comes up with all kinds of creations. I usually get a new one every month."

Mia stopped to read the label and admire the jar before taking in the smell. "Vanilla Smiles? Interesting. I thought the smell was lavender."

"Yeah, I thought the same thing. I guess if we were candle manufacturers, we'd have known that." Darren flashed a quick smile then clapped his hands together. "So, what's up? You letting me give Mari some pointers or what?"

"Yeah, that's what I wanted to talk to you about," Mia said hesitantly.

"What, you need a background investigation?" Darren joked.

Mia was a little embarrassed, because she knew she was overreacting, but at the same time, this was her brother they were talking about. "No, but," Mia stammered. "I guess there's no way to say it other than just to say it."

"You're starting to worry me, Amia Copeland." Darren sat on the edge of his desk and motioned for Mia to have a seat. "Please. Say what's on your mind."

"Ok, Darren, please don't be offended, but I kind of know you, from our time here and everyone's talk about your camp and your relationship with the kids, but I don't really *know you, know you*. I just kind of need to understand a little more about you, if that's okay. Does that make sense?"

"Yes ma'am, it does. You know, I've got some pretty good references that I can provide you with," Darren joked, tipping his head toward the picture on the shelf showing him with the three partners.

"Darren...I'm serious, this is my little brother." Mia laughed. "I've just got to make sure that I'm making the right decisions for him. You understand that, right?"

"Alright, alright, big sis, sheesh." Darren took a breath and scratched his thick, short goatee. "Alright, without going into everything, I was Jamari Copeland twenty years ago. I found myself chest-deep in some major shit. The difference is that I didn't have a big sister or a team of people who'd have walked through hell for me.

"My parents were both hard-core thugs. They'd been in the drug game for years and always told me that if anything ever happened to them that my sisters and I would be sent to foster care and would never see each other again.

"One night, two guys came to the house wanting drugs. My mom and dad took them back to the office," Darren continued, making air quotes as he said 'office'. "Less than a minute later, there was yelling. You could hear stuff being thrown around and the next thing you know, there were 6 gunshots. Thankfully, my sisters were at the skating rink with their friends that night. I hid behind the sofa waiting for the guys to come out.

"I just figured that my parents were dead and I was next, but that's not what happened. My parents came out. Both were a little frazzled, but not nearly shaken enough to have just had been attacked and shot at. They were trying to figure out how to get rid of the drugs and money and at the same time figuring out how to get rid of the bodies.

"After hearing my dad call my name, I crawled from behind the couch. He asked me what I'd seen and heard and then *told* me what I'd actually seen and heard. He then told me how things went down and what needed to be done. The next day, my mom called 9-1-1 to say that I had killed two men that had broken into our house.

"I didn't want my parents to go to jail because I didn't want to be split up from my sisters, so I confessed to having shot them. My dad convinced me that the police would believe my story and everything would be okay. What I didn't know is that my previous two infractions would be factored. My dad knew it, but I didn't. When I was giving my statement, the lead detective came in with my book bag chocked full of heroin. Of course, it wasn't mine, but I couldn't tell them who it belonged to.

Darren shrugged, walked to a window, and continued, "The police didn't believe my story from the start. They didn't believe the home invasion thing. They decided that I'd called them over to the house and killed them in cold blood. I learned later that to remove themselves further from the police investigation, my parents had told them that *I* was a dope dealer and that they'd been struggling to get *me* on track."

Darren half-chuckled in reply to Mia's stunned expression. "It's crazy, right? They told them that I had been talking for a couple of days about smoking some rival dealers.

"And to seal the deal, at the end of a one-on-one visit with my father, he hugged me and warned that if I tried changing my story, he'd kill my mom and my sisters. I'd actually seen my dad stomp his small-time dealers for not hustling hard enough, stab a junkie for grabbing his coat, and kill two rival dealers, so I knew he was capable of making good on that threat. I felt like a non-English-speaking foreigner who'd lost his wallet in Manhattan — lost and absolutely petrified. I didn't want to go to jail. I didn't want to die, and I wanted my family to be safe.

"Sorry, hang on one sec. Yes Janel," he replied in response to the secretary's buzz.

"Hi Darren, Patricia White is returning your call. She's on line four."

"Thank you. Ask her to hold for a minute, please. I'm wrapping up something."

Mia was already on her feet heading towards the door. She was dumbstruck and at an utter loss for words.

"Darren. I. . . I don't know what to say." She knew she didn't need to offer comfort because it had been decades since this happened. But she still grappled to find something useful to contribute after Darren's incredibly personal disclosure.

He assured her that it was okay. Everyone at the firm knew his story. "So, Ms. Copeland, can I coach your little brother?"

"Absolutely. Who knew you held that kind of past behind that smile?"

"You just never know, do you?" he replied, with all thirty-two pearlies on full display adorned artfully by two deep dimples.

"Thank you for taking an interest in Jamari. I already respected you, but Oh. My. God!"

"Well, you know. When life gives you lemons, you hope there are a bunch of people around you who know how to make lemonade."

Mia now understood exactly why he always said that.

A few minutes later, Mia was thumbing through the camp authorizations, releases, and other paperwork with a completely new appreciation for her incredibly handsome colleague and renewed adoration for her beloved law firm.

CHAPTER 9:
JULY 2000
In a Word – SAVED

"SCHOOL'S BEEN OUT for almost four weeks. You finished the semester A's and B's –"

"Except for that C in Geometry," Mari added. "Mr. Boyd really could have given me a 79.5 then it could have been rounded up to a B."

"You got a 79.4% in the class. Was Mr. Boyd supposed to pull that extra tenth out of the sky and give it to you? I don't think so," retorted Officer Michaels before continuing, "Earn the B next time and you don't have to worry about anyone giving you anything," retorted Officer Michaels. "Great job though "You're heading to the ninth grade now, right?"

"Yes."

"I'm proud of you and you should be proud of yourself. Not too bad for a kid who was selling drugs just fifteen months ago."

"Thank you, Officer."

"No problem. So, you've satisfied the terms of your parole. You don't have to see me anymore. If we bump into each other, cool, but *I don't want to have to see you again*," he said matter-of-factly. "Understand?"

"Yes, Sir. I don't want to see you again either . . . I mean, respectfully, though," Mari added placing his hands over his chest and smiling.

"May the road rise to meet you, Son. Take care of yourself and her," Officer Michaels said nodding in Mia's direction.

"For sure, Sir. You don't have to worry about that."

"Thank you Officer Michaels," added Mia hugging the 30-year police veteran while reflecting on the advice and tough talk that he'd provided Mari over the past year.

On their way back from his final check-in Mari reflected on his life since leaving Lancaster. He had so many positive role models surrounding him on a regular basis. He didn't have room or time to get off course. He'd made the varsity team thanks to Darren's camp and one-on-one attention.

Marty, Mike and Geoff continued letting Mari sit in on their research and discovery meetings. Mia would let him assist her with researching old case files to look for different angles, surprise verdicts, and interesting defense tactics.

When they were at home, the pair jammed to the latest songs on the radio while making dinner and always ate together at the table while discussing their days, the weather, siblings, or anything that came to mind. Mia would even let him practice pickup lines and small talk for the opposite sex.

Mari also loved church. He'd been going for almost six months before giving his life to Christ. He reflected on that moment during a one-on-one with Darren earlier in the year . . .

"What if God's not real?"

Mari had been holding onto that question for months but didn't know who he could trust with that inquiry. He hadn't gone to church at all in Lancaster. While his parents referenced the Lord, he'd never really understood who He was. Because Mari knew that Mia loved God, he figured she'd be worried if he asked her. Mari also decided that he couldn't ask the people at church because as nice as they were, they might be offended. With that, he asked the one person that he trusted with the good, the bad, and the ugly – Darren.

"Why do you ask that?"

"I don't know. I mean, you can't hear Him or see Him and bad stuff happens all the time. Why would God let babies and good people die?"

"Those are good questions. You definitely should ask Him," Darren smiled.

"Listen, Mari. I know there's a God because we are sitting here having this conversation. I'm supposed to be in prison or dead. You could very well be locked up yourself.

"Bad things are going to happen. It's a part of life. Bad things happened to Jesus and He is God's son. Truth is that Satan got kicked out of Heaven and is spending his days trying to make people as miserable as he is. He's trying to steal their joy and have them live a life not knowing God. Those people will end up with him in the lake of fire. He wants to keep us from knowing God, receiving his blessings and having everlasting life.

"Think about this. What if Mia wasn't old enough to be able to take you in. Where would you be? What if my parents hadn't hung me out to dry? Would I have met Geoff, Marty & Mike? What if she didn't work at WW&M? Would you and I know each other? What if you hadn't wanted to play football? Would I be out here with you today? The answer to all of those questions is no.

"There are no coincidences, Mari. All of this is coordinated by God. He knows everything that has and ever will happen to all of us – and He cares. The bible says in Matthew 10:29 that not even a little sparrow can hit the ground without God knowing. Think about that. A little sparrow. You know how many birds are in the world? Now, if He knows what's up with a sparrow, He's definitely got us.

"Yeah, there is going to be rain and pain, but we just have to keep the faith and He will bring us through."

"Does God forgive everything?" Mari asked, his voice twinged with guilt.

"I think there's only one or two things that He ain't having. What's up?"

"Promise you won't say anything?"

Darren put his arm on his shoulder almost searching his soul. "Mari, talk to me."

"I don't know . . . never mind," he said looking away.

"Hey, listen to me. I have two sisters. I always prayed for a little brother as I was growing up and suddenly here you are. So, in case you're still wondering if God is real, He is — very much so.

"Mari, talk to me. What's on your mind?"

Mari smiled and hugged Darren and while they were the only two in the area, he whispered his secret during their embrace. Darren hugged him hard and assured him that he was good and just had to ask the Lord for forgiveness.

"Ok, I'll ask on Sunday when I go to church."

"Why wait? You can ask for forgiveness right now. You don't have to wait to go to church. The church isn't the building. It's inside of you once you ask Jesus to come into your heart. You want to do that too?"

"Right here?"

"Looks like a great place to me," Darren replied looking around and smiling. With that, he led Jamari in the prayer of salvation — the most important prayer he'd ever pray.

"Repeat after me. Father God, please forgive me of my sins. I believe that Jesus died for my sins, rose again on the third day and is alive with all power. Please Jesus come into my heart and become Lord of my life from this day forward. Father, please send your Holy Spirit to help me obey You and to do Your will for the rest of my life. Amen."

"You good," asked Darren. "How do you feel?"

"It's weird . . . I don't know. It's like my insides are happy," replied Mari fumbling for the right words.

"Yeah, that's called the joy of the Lord. You've got that now."

"Will it stay? I mean, will I always be happy?"

"Maybe. Maybe not, but it will always be there for you to tap into. We're gonna leave this park and Mia's probably gonna fuss at you for not picking up your shoes. You might get irritated, but now you can control how you respond because of that joy that lives inside."

"Ok, I get that," Mari added.

"But will God still love me when I mess up?"

"Bruh, God doesn't expect perfection. He *created* us. He *knows* we're not perfect. In fact, He already knows your next move. Listen, Mari. The only perfect man walked this Earth thousands of years ago and I know there hasn't been another Jesus. It's our job to live our lives in a way that brings Him glory and to let others see Him in us. When we fall short, we ask Him for forgiveness and try not to do it again. At the end of the day, when our time here is up, we want to get to Heaven and hear God say, "Well done, thy good and faithful servant".

"There's not a magic formula or special trick to

being a Christian. Just try to be the best person you can be. Talk to God. He's got you. And know that you can't make Him stop loving you, no matter what you do."

The two embraced for a few moments more before finishing up their workout.

CHAPTER 10:
MAY 2002
In a Word – THRIVING

SHORTLY AFTER HIS arrival in Pittsburgh Mia discovered that Mari not only liked yardwork – he was really good at it. He had cut her lawn into a checkerboard pattern and her edges were sculpted to perfection. Mia's flowerbeds no longer featured the latest dandelions and crabgrass poking through patches of rock. Now, her townhome boasted curb appeal with bursts of colorful annuals and fresh black mulch. She was happy that Mari convinced her to purchase the butterfly wind chime as its thin metal rods created the softest pleasant ringing when kissed by the wind. Her yard now truly echoed the harmony, effort and love that abounded inside their home.

"Mari, why don't you ask the neighbors if they'd like you to do their yards every week or every other week? That way, you could earn more than your current allowance. I knew you cut the grass back at home, but I always thought that Mr. Pearson handled the landscaping. You're actually really good at this."

"You think anyone would go for that?"

Mia jokingly, but seriously continued, "Um yeah. My yard is all the advertising you need for this neighborhood. Everyone knows what it looked like last year. All they have to do is compare today's yard to that one and you're all set."

Conveniently, the next morning was a Saturday. Mari had gotten out bright and early knocking on doors charging an introductory price of $15 for the front and back yard. He returned home that evening exhausted and sun burnt, but $235 richer. He averaged $40 per home after the owners surveyed his mowing and edging skills capped off by his weeding and even freshening their mulch beds. Since that day, whenever he was not at football camp, church, or work with Mia, J&M's Landscaping was open for business.

Mia was so relieved that he'd found a way to make good, honest money. She'd seen how he longingly looked at the designer sneakers and clothes when they went to the mall. Though he had many positive influences around him, Mia did worry about whether her little brother would be able to resist the allure of fast money.

ELAINE, SHAMIR, BRIA, and Jordyn called twice a week to talk to Mari and Mia. The pair loved talking to the kids about their activities and listening to Bria and Jordyn wrestle over who would talk first. They visited each other twice a month alternating the drives.

Though it never really surfaced, there was an underlying tension between Mari & Elaine. As happy as he was with his life with Mia, he couldn't help but feel slighted because Elaine – in his opinion – gave up on him. In addition, he learned that Elaine had stopped working so much and started being at home with the kids more. He wondered why he had to get into so much trouble for her to remember her family.

Mari still felt the loss of not having Ramon in his life. His feelings of abandonment would come and go – though were always present when he and Mia would visit their old home. They were also especially pervasive whenever he was on the football field. While all players had a pregame ritual, Mari's included a full-blown pep talk from his uniform-clad reflection. If he squinted hard enough or the lighting was just right, the helmeted athlete in the mirror actually could pass for Ramon.

"Mari," 'Ramon' would say.

"No ball that the quarterback throws tonight will be a

50/50 chance. If he's throwing to you, it's 100/0 chance. You *will* catch it. The defender *will not*. Again, *you will* catch it. The defender *will not*. I believe in you, Son."

While this was a personal conversation with his dad, he would always say this in the voice of a loud southern Baptist preacher. The preacher's voice allowed the words to ring through his chest, but also kept the atmosphere light enough for his listening teammates. On top of that, it allowed him to repeat the pep-talk several times before bursting through the corridor and onto the field with his team.

The dull ache from knowing that Ramon wouldn't be in the stands was always there. Sure, there were plenty of people cheering him on, including the staff of WW&M during his first home game as a starter, but it wasn't the same as having Ramon there.

Mia would talk with Mari about his feelings sometimes, but Mari mainly confided his deepest hurts in Darren. If there was ever anything shared that was alarming, Darren would loop in Mia. Otherwise, she just had to trust that Darren was being the big brother offering good guidance to Mari.

The full family weekends were all the same – a combination of fried chicken, pork chops or spaghetti and Elaine's famous dressing atop a massive salad comprised of every fruit and vegetable known to man. This was always wrapped around plenty of good conversation. Jordyn always wanted to be measured, insisting that she'd grown at least two inches since their last visit and one dared to dispute that little one. After all, with her spit fire, all agreed that this was a battle best not waged.

Shamir chatted up the latest sports scores and who's who in the sports world. Much to his chagrin, Elaine would always mention the latest little girl who was crushing on him. Bria would always add that another one of her classmates said he was cute. "Poor Shamir." Laughed Mari. "He's completely outnumbered." Bria, the Copeland brain, always summarized her latest homework assignments and explained why she received the scores she got. During their last visit, Elaine reported that she'd been called to the school to console a sobbing Bria. When she saw Mia & Mari's confused looks, Bria defended her position.

"I got an A- on my book report on The Hobbit. I deserved an A+ because I worked extra hard and even colored a picture of each main character on the cover. Nobody else drew everybody on their cover and Mikey Adams got an A and he didn't even color any of his characters. So I should have definitely got an A+." It was clear that Mikey's A irked Bria because her arms folded across her chest as soon as she uttered his name.

Mia and Mari's jaws dropped and they looked at each other, then Elaine.

"Don't look at me. She was sure her cover alone was worth the A+ and the fact that 'others' did not go the extra mile . . . Let's just say someone was unhappy," mouthed Elaine.

"I might just call Mrs. Roberts and have a chat with her. How about that?" asked Mia.

Shamicka C. Toney

"Nah, Mia. It's cool. Brie, you know what?" added Mari. "I bet she thought that if you got an A+ on your first book report that you wouldn't try as hard on your next one. I bet you'll get that A+ next time."

Bria lit up. "You think so?"

"I dunno." Shrugged Elaine. "But one thing's for sure, Ms. Roberts knows you're serious about your book reports."

———~———

"I'M GOING TO the grocery store. Mari, you want to ride with me?" This was Elaine's way of getting time alone with him. None of the other kids liked grocery shopping and anyways, they preferred to hang out at Mia's townhouse while Elaine and Mari went out. During each of their outings, Elaine would stop for ice cream or a burger and she and Mari would catch up.

Though Mari enjoyed spending the one-on-one time with Elaine, the conversations – from Mari's perspective – often missed the mark. He desperately wanted to understand why she had to work as much as she had when he lived there but has now scaled

94

back and hadn't suffered at all financially. He longed to know why she'd tossed him to the side so quickly, but he could never find the courage to ask. Instead, he'd always tell her about school and life with Mia and made sure that Elaine knew he was doing the right thing and was happy.

Elaine would always tell him how proud she was of the job he was doing and to keep it up. They'd always wrap up their two-hour outings with a stop at the grocery store to pick up fruit and some leafy green veggies to ensure that their "grocery store" excursions were always seen as boring. They'd always return without candy, chips, or toys just to ensure that they were never in danger of having party crashers.

On the other hand, Mom/Son conversations back in Lancaster were always held at the Copeland family home. Neither Elaine, Mia, nor Mari was interested in having anyone know he was in town — by anyone, that meant his past affiliates. Mari had decided that he was in a better place and didn't want to be bothered with that element anymore.

He did miss the fast money though. He often reminisced about how quickly he could make $50. But Mari also remembered how things were in that world. He remembered what happened to anyone who crossed a dealer or didn't supply a client who was tweaking. He remembered all too well how many times he'd been threatened. And since Mari's only reason for getting involved with dealing drugs in the first place was to help his mom, he didn't have any interest in ever going there again.

Besides, Mari's life was great now. Everyone liked him. He'd made the varsity team as an eighth grader. He was happy, making good friends, excelling in school and was probably the only teenager around helping out with court cases. He was surrounded by cool, positive, men of various nationalities – all of whom were educated and had great jobs or owned businesses. To quote the teens, the men had nice whips, phat cribs, mad gear, and major bling.

The one thing that constantly impressed Mari with all the men in his life was that none of them were involved in anything illegal. No one was running or hiding, no one was threatening murder, and no one really cursed. The only other man in Mari's life who he knew like that (minus the cursing) was Ramon.

For Mari, out of all the men he's recently come to know, Darren Wilford was by far his favorite. Sure, he loved hanging with Brother Simpson at their church and enjoyed the attention of all of his mentors, but Darren understood him more than any of the others. Mari could talk to Darren about anything because it felt to him like Darren knew exactly where he was coming from.

CHAPTER 11:
In a Word – LIFTED

"**I** TOLD YOU THAT you didn't have to pay for any dry cleaning, Darren. It was an accident."

"Don't worry about it," he replied while insisting she take the money. "I just hate that I left that mug sitting so close to the edge. You would have been burned really badly, if it had still been hot. It's the least I could do."

Mia reluctantly took the cash and since she had no pockets, set it under her coffee cup on Darren's desk and resumed pouring through case notes.

They were six weeks away from the start of Morris Chesterson's trial. He was a sixty-one-year-old single grandfather who'd been charged with first-degree murder. Darren agreed to take on his case at the behest of his Pastor. As he scoured the man's background investigation, Darren noted that Morris had worked at Klattville Juvenile Detention Center – the same Klattville Detention Center that he'd spent time in as a child.

"Isn't that ironic," he said. His demeanor almost stoic.

Mia reminded him that he'd never finished the story that he'd started almost a year ago – prior to his coaching Jamari. She confessed that she'd always been curious about the rest of the story but hadn't found the right opportunity to revisit the conversation.

"Yeah, sure. I could use a break. Want a refill?"

Before Mia could reply, he'd scooped her cup and made the corner into the hallway.

Upon his return, he extend the piping hot cup of Joe to Mia. "Two creams and one sugar, right?"

"Yes, thanks," said Mia quite intrigued that he'd remembered.

"I think Janel buzzed in as I was telling you about my dad threatening to kill my mom and sisters, right?" Mia was again curious that he'd remembered exactly where the story ended almost a year ago. It seemed that she wasn't the only one who was trying to find the right moment to reengage.

"Good memory," she managed.

"Gotta stay sharp," he replied jokingly.

As Darren resumed his story, Mia forced herself to dismiss the rising flattery that had been steadily creeping in and threatening to show up in her body language.

"Alright. So basically, I was looking at being tried as an adult with consecutive life sentences and no possibility of parole. What saved me was the media attention," Darren recalled while sipping the fresh brew from his mug.

"Four months into my confinement at Klattville, Geoff walked in." Darren placed his coffee on his desk, put his hands in his pockets and looked up slowly. "I was fourteen and completely broken. I had been set up by my parents and my dad had threatened to kill my family if I told the truth. There was no light to be found anywhere.

"Geoff saw a good kid in the most unimaginable situation. The partners never did believe my story, but I stuck with it until the day before trial. I kept asking to see pictures of my sisters, so they recorded a video of my sisters playing at the playground. I saw how big my baby sister had gotten and I broke down completely. I told them everything – what really happened."

Darren looked up at the ceiling and shook his head. "They fought tooth and nail to make me tell the truth in court." Darren smiled remembering the earnest influencing tactics that they'd employed on him back then, and continued, "It was absolutely not happening. I was too afraid that my dad would follow through.

"Geoff and Marty were able to get a continuance and worked with the DEA to set up a sting. Unfortunately, my mom got caught too, and that was a problem because I knew if she went to prison, we kids would be separated and would never see each other again. So, what did I do? Clammed right back up. I wasn't saying anything else.

"About three days later, Geoff finally got me to tell

him what else was going on in my mind. Because my mom and dad were high rollers and were implicated in multiple other murders, the DEA pulled all kinds of strings with the District Attorney and Child Services. They worked with the foster system to get my sisters put in the same home. They also assured me that if I was acquitted, I could come home with them.

"Ultimately, the charges against me were dropped. About a year later, my folks went on trial. They had every charge in the book. My mom ultimately took a plea in exchange for testifying against my dad. She got 39 years without the possibility of parole. My dad's trial lasted four weeks. There were dozens of witnesses. I remember being on the stand for three days utterly terrified every minute. The Jury deliberated for five hours and came back with the guilty verdict. My father was sentenced to six consecutive life sentences."

He then pointed to a well-framed 10 x 13 photo. In it was an older Caucasian couple smiling with him in his cap and gown. In the picture, the threesome was flanked by Darren's younger sisters. Mia had seen the image several times and was curious about the pair.

"I spent the next five years with Mable & Gary Felding, my foster parents. They were Godsends for me and my sisters." He then smiled at Mia and added, "They still are.

"Geoff, Marty, and Mike kept in touch with me over the years. They gave me part-time jobs here at the firm every summer and Mike's brother, the football pro bowler, let me go to his football camps every year.

"So, that's it. I think it's also why I'm so drawn to Jamari. In many ways, I see myself in him. Granted, my life was a lot rougher than his, but I'm pretty positive that I understand him more than anyone else."

"Darren, I'm so sorry you had to endure that. I really am. . . Wow," she added shaking her head.

"It's all good. Like I said, it was a long time ago. There's been plenty of lemonade since," he added with a thoughtful smile. Could you hand me that yellow folder please?"

Mia handed him the accordion-style packet and as the pair continued pouring through the mountains of police reports and witness statements, she silently wondered how he'd coped during that time. She wondered how lonely and afraid that fourteen-year old must have been. She wanted to know how he dealt with his anger. What was it like learning that he had no one in his corner? How did he stay sane? She ached for that little boy tucked safely inside this powerful man. Mia surmised that his unrelenting fight for his clients was directly related to his experience as an abandoned teenager in Klattville.

CHAPTER 12:
In a Word – PERPLEXED

"**I**'M TAKING THE girls to Hershey Park next weekend," Mia reminded Marty before leaving the office for Memorial Day weekend.

By "the girls," Mia had been referring to Marty's three daughters – Faith, Chrystal, and Trinity. All three were teenagers and loved hanging out with Mia. Unfortunately, spending time with the girls regularly was one of the sacrifices Mia had to make once Mari moved in. Marty and his wife, Victoria, made sure to bring the girls to the office at least once per week so that they got to see her. The more she thought about it, the more excited Mia was about spending the day at Hershey Park with them.

She was the girls' idol. She was everything every little girl wanted to be – smart and funny, owned a home and a car. She had a great job, made good money, and had the biggest personality amplified by an utterly amazing smile. In addition, Mia was tall, with beautiful oval eyes and thick hair cut into a shoulder-length bob and had even-toned deep brown skin.

Mia wasn't Barbie doll skinny either. At 5'10", she was a healthy size twelve. She would eat a large Value Meal or a six-inch veggie sub. It really depended on her mood. She would also exercise maybe 3 - 4 times per week. There was nothing about her that was forced or overdone. Mia didn't wear much makeup and was rarely glammed up. She just had an easy natural beauty that was enhanced with eyeliner, mascara and lip gloss. Truth be told, that was more than Mia needed, but she did want to look older than eighteen while at work.

Interestingly enough, Mia was always asked if she was the girls' older sister due to them having some similarities. Each of the girls was tall and fairly lanky with thick hair and full, inviting smiles. Mia and the youngest, Trinity, both had birthmarks on their shoulder blades, so Mia allowed the girls to playfully answer yes.

"MIA, HELLO, MIA?"

"Huh?" she replied without looking up from her

plate. She'd barely acknowledged her dinner date — now good friend, Darren. Though their relationship was completely platonic, Mia spent a lot of time with him. From Mari's first practices at Darren's camp and the one-on-one trainings years ago, they'd been grabbing coffee, lunch, or dinner from time to time.

She often thought of having a relationship with him, but, again, workplace romances were strictly off limits. At this point, they were such good friends that Mia didn't want to cross that line. Though she had to admit that there had been many times when she wanted to have Darren stay over for a very different kind of one-on-one.

Besides the notion of potentially ruining their friendship and messing up her career at the firm, Mia was insistent about practicing what she preached to Mari. Sure, she'd dated other men, but had never once let anyone stay overnight nor did she stay out past her self-imposed midnight curfew.

"Mia, you've been acting weird ever since your weekend at Hershey Park with the girls. What gives?" The concern in Darren's voice made Mia look up from her vegetable lasagna to meet his dark eyes. His jaw clenched reflecting his concern.

Darren's taut jaw combined with his dark, slightly furrowed eyebrows was inspiring intensely naughty thoughts. Again, Mia wouldn't dare go there with him, but she was a woman. She briefly imagined herself kicking out all the other patrons and ravishing his beautiful body right there on top their linen-clad table in retaliation for his being so ridiculously sexy. But as immense as her desire for Darren's embrace was, Mia really needed her companion to give her an answer that made sense. She took a sip of her freckled lemonade and started thinking about how to share what had been eating her for the past few days.

"Darren, we bumped into the girls' uncle, Maxwell, while we were at Hershey Park. Remember him, he's Marty's older brother. The girls didn't introduce me. They didn't really say much to him other than hi."

"Yeah, I remember Maxwell. He's a drunk and a clown. Remember he came to the office a couple years ago asking Marty for $100.00 and then destroyed the lobby when Marty kicked him out. Marty has a restraining order against that fool."

"I know and since the girls weren't interested in having conversation or hanging around, I decided to move us along. I'd planned to tell Marty that we'd bumped into Maxwell when I dropped the girls off or when he called to check on them."

"Ok, so why is that bothering you so much?"

"No, it wasn't that, Darren. As we were leaving, he told me to say hi to Elaine and called me his baby girl."

"Wait, what? How does he know your mom? And why would he call you his baby girl? That dude is straight stupid." Darren's eyebrow arched, nostrils flared, and jaw clenched. Each of them reflecting anger.

"I see why Marty doesn't deal with him," he snorted. "That brotha's a straight idiot." Taking another sip of his Heineken, Darren asked, "Has your mom ever mentioned him?"

"That's just it. Mom and Dad had been living together for a few years prior to getting married and as far as I know, they were high school sweethearts and madly in love. They'd always been together. Right up to the divorce."

Mia was struggling to wrap her head around what Maxwell had said. Standing suddenly, she had an unnerving thought that rattled into a slew of questions. "Is it possible that my mom cheated on my dad? Is the reason that everyone thinks I'm one of Marty's children because I'm actually his niece? Am I that naive? Why wouldn't Marty say anything to me?"

"Whoa, whoa, Mia. Take a breath. You can't take anything that that knucklehead says to heart.

"I wouldn't lose any sleep over him, but if you want, ask your mom and Marty about that fool's rant. Mia, we both know Marty would do anything for you and I'm pretty sure that if he knew something, he'd have told you or at least have dropped a hint. Especially with your researching skills." Darren winked.

They finished up the meal chatting about Mia's latest find which resulted in a mistrial this week and about three of Darren's campers who'd recently earned top national honors and now have their choice of the top colleges and universities in the nation.

In the parking lot, the two friends hugged and Darren kissed her forehead as he did at the end of each outing.

Because Darren shared Mia's feelings of intimacy and workplace romances, a kiss on the forehead was all that he could handle. He'd learned early on that Mia's cheek was way too close to the suppleness of her soft, slightly glossed lips. Her cheek was also far too close to her long, slender neck which was always subtlety spritzed with some intoxicating perfume. He'd even asked Addie to make a candle with the fragrance. That one, unbeknownst to Mia, has been kept at his immaculately designed condo. The place where deep down, he'd longed to have her call home.

After breaking the hug, Darren grinned and asked Mia if her weekend plans included a trip to Lancaster.

"You know it," she said smiling back. "Do you mind if Mari hangs –."

"One step ahead of you. I knew you weren't sticking around when you started telling me about Max's ignorant ass. He hasn't seen Spider Man 2 yet, right? Yes!" He exclaimed after Mia shook her head. "I was hoping you'd say that. I've been wanting to see it but haven't had a chance and I didn't want to be that weird grown man in the theater all by myself. We'll catch the movie. I'll spank Mari's behind at bowling – again – and we'll go to church on Sunday. I'll make sure he gets his homework done. It'll be great."

"Thanks, D, you're a sweetie." Mia sighed giving him another hug and inhaling a full whiff of his Drakkar scented masculinity before stepping into Goldie.

"No problem, Mama. You know, you can look into replacing Goldie any time now. She's got over 100,000 miles on her. You need something with a more reliable engine since you're always traveling up and down the highway."

"...traveling up and down the highway," Mia said simultaneously. She'd heard Darren, Marty, Mike, and Geoff all say that more times than she cared to remember.

Goldie was Mia's baby. Everyone knew it was her first purchase as an adult and she just wasn't ready to part with her. Besides, Mari would be seventeen soon and would need a car. Goldie would be perfect for him. "I told you, I'm keeping my baby. Now, stop talking about Goldie before you hurt her feelings," Mia added smiling before turning to step into the vehicle.

"Oh, and your girl knows more about that robbery at her grandmother's house than she's telling you."

"Who? Maureen?"

"Yes, Maureen."

Darren continued holding the door though Mia changed her mind about getting in. He casually leaned against Goldie while eying Mia quizzically. He inhaled deeply, shutting his eyes in anticipation of the bombshell that was surely coming. "Alright, Ms. Copeland. I'm listening."

"In her statement, Maureen told investigators that she left the house around 8:30 after eating something that made her sick. She said that she was throwing up and had diarrhea. Maureen then stated she had to go to the drug store to pick up some medicine because she couldn't find any at her grandmother's house."

"Right, the video we pulled showed her at the register at 8:40 buying the Pepto and some gum."

"Yes it does. But, something wasn't sitting right with me, so I went through the videos and evidence photos again this afternoon. In the video of her coming into the station to give her statement that night, her purse was open. There was a shiny object in there that caught my eye, so I had a still photo taken and enlarged the image. That shiny thing turned out to be a wrapper. You wanna guess what kind of wrapper?"

"Enlighten me, Ms. Copeland."

"It was the wrapper on the Pepto bottle. She never opened it. I don't know about you, but if my stomach had been as rumbly as she said hers was, I'd have taken that Pepto right there in the parking lot of the drug store. Instead, Maureen drove back home, found the ransacked house, called 9-1-1, waited for the police, and then went to the station – all without ever opening the bottle."

"Come on. Seriously?" Darren sighed burying his forehead in his hand. "You're right, that doesn't make any sense at all." He then faced Mia searching her amazing eyes for any sign of uncertainty. After not finding any, he continued. "You're absolutely sure it wasn't open, Amia?"

"That seal appears to be fully intact around the bottle. The drug store video only shows her buying one bottle of Pepto. Darren, I know you believe her, but ask yourself why someone who was so nauseated and violently ill would risk leaving the house and driving a few blocks to get the medicine, but not take it?" Mia then tapped the arm of her befuddled friend before hopping into and cranking up Goldie.

"Interestingly though, the photos show an open pack of Juicy Fruit gum with a stick missing. I'm willing to bet it matches the piece that was found on the floor of that house. Remember, Maureen also told the investigators that the gum had fallen out of her mouth when she screamed. But again, if her stomach was so upset, why eat the gum, but not take the Pepto?"

Darren smiled while shaking his head incredulously. "You're good, Ms. Copeland. Really, really good."

"I left the photos and a copy of her statement on your desk. You probably want to ask her about that before the Prosecution does." Mia winked at her cutie pie buddy and headed home.

"MAN, I SWEAR nothing's going on," exclaimed Darren while riding home and cancelling his weekend plans with Todd so that he could look after Mari. Todd was one of his oldest friends. "Why you keep bringing up Arturo's? I swear that was nothing," Darren insisted while half grinning. "Look, she was out with her male friend and I was out with my female friend. It wasn't a big deal."

"Yeah, Ok. Man, you looked like a sick puppy when Mia stepped into that restaurant modeling that red spaghetti strapped blouse and those thigh-high shorts."

Darren broke into a full-throated laughter.

"Man, you straight stupid. You ain't got no sense," he'd exclaimed still laughing at his college buddy while hiding the fact that it was true. Darren had been envious of her date's unbelievable luck and had even found himself sizing the brotha up in case he'd even thought about stepping out of line.

CHAPTER 13:
In a Word – QUESTIONS

"**T**HAT'S RIGHT, ASK Jerome if we can meet at five o'clock today. I just had something pressing come up that I need to handle... Hmmm, okay. Well, I'm also free all morning tomorrow if we can't make 5:00 work. Just put it on the schedule for me. Thanks...Oh, Janel, can you hold all calls for me for the next forty-five minutes? Thanks."

"Thanks for carving out some time for me."

"Mia, you've only asked me for my undivided attention a few times. Once was for Mari and the other two led to huge acquittals. So, no problem. What's up?"

"Marty, I haven't slept well for the past several days. I'm heading to Lancaster tomorrow because I'm confused."

"Why aren't you sleeping? What's bothering you?" Marty put his hand on hers and searched her sunken, exhausted eyes for clues. Everyone was in fast-forward this past week, trying to secure final evidence in their upcoming money laundering appeal case. This was his first time really seeing her since last week. Marty also noticed that her clothes were hanging a bit loosely.

"If you knew something about someone close to you that would turn their life upside down, would you tell them?" She looked at him intensely and then looked down at her hands which were fidgeting in her lap.

"It depends on who and what the information is. You can never just answer that question one way...Mia, I'm getting worried. Please tell me what's going on."

"Marty, I ran into Maxwell last weekend."

"Yeah, the girls told me." Marty rolled his eyes. "Are you going to tell me that he's not really my brother?" He joked. Then apologized for interrupting.

Mia chuckled. "Yeah, right." She then sighed. "Marty, do you know how he would know my mom?"

"Did he say that he did?"

"Not only did he say that he knew her, he called me his baby girl."

Marty's light skin began quickly turning pink then red as his temperature steadily rose. Mia had seen him angry, but his hue was starting to match his striped ruby button-down shirt. "Mia, I love him because he's my brother, but that drunk bastard has nothing better to do than spout stupid crap." Marty was absolutely seething. "Maybe he's adding drugs back into his recreational equation now. I guess alcohol no longer does it for him." Marty spat.

"I can't wrap my mind around it either, Marty. He's never met my mother. Did you mention her around him? And why would he call me his baby girl? He doesn't know me either."

"I'll tell you this much, I was so impressed with you when you came that I told a lot of people about you. After you started working cases, you started making a name for yourself. People can look you up on the internet now. I guess someone could trace your genealogy, but I do know that I haven't said anything to Max. We haven't talked like that in years."

"Do you mind me asking what happened between you two?"

"All that I'll say is that being a star basketball player in college gave him the big head. He became too good for anyone and too high on himself to listen to good advice. It was like he got to California and lost his mind. By the time he completed his freshman year, he'd been in four fights.

"In his sophomore year, he had a sexual assault accusation which was dropped and had failed two drug tests. In his junior year, he was arrested for rape. The victim didn't want to go through with the trial. Ultimately, Max pleaded guilty to sexual battery from the freshman year incident and served two years' probation. By that time, the university had had enough of his insolence and 1.53 GPA. They were uninterested in standing by him – much less seeing in him in their jersey on national TV. His scholarship was revoked and Max was ultimately thrown out of school.

"I was a freshman in college when Max got expelled and moved back home. As a convicted sex offender, he couldn't get a real job and there were no more colleges offering to pay his way. He started drinking, smoking, and running with the wrong crowd. It just spiraled from there.

"When I was a junior at Stanford, I brought Victoria home to introduce her to the family. That visit ended up with him getting kicked out of Weeboy for groping Vicky's derrière when she went to wash her hands." Marty shook his head and continued, "You probably didn't get a good look at Max, but there are two scars on his head. One at the hairline and one on his chin. Vicky gave him the one on his chin. Her engagement ring — that I'd just given her — caught him when she whirled around to take that joker's teeth out. The other scar was from the gash that opened on his head when he stumbled backwards from the blow and hit his head against the baseboard.

"Yep," he continued in response to Mia's astonished expression. "That brotha got seven stitches in his chin and twelve in his scalp for copping a feel. I knew right then that I'd better not ever mess up! Truth be told, because of how she jacked him up, I was too afraid to call off the wedding even if I'd wanted to. Shooottt, the way she hemmed him up, I knew I'd have earned a plot for even thinking of pulling anything over on her!" Both Marty and Mia had a hearty laugh at that one.

"Seriously, Mia. Max isn't worth it. You know that 'baby girl' is just an expression these young dudes say to a female that they're interested in. I wouldn't miss another night's sleep or any more meals over it."

She immediately knew what he meant by missing meals. Her appetite was completely gone. Who could think about food with all of this madness?

"Marty, he didn't call me baby girl. His exact words were, 'My baby girl.' I could be letting my imagination run away from me, but is it possible? I mean, everyone thinks I'm your child because we favor and I look like your girls."

"A-mi-a Cope-land!" Marty scolded.

"Number one, all Black people look alike in some way, shape, or form. We all happen to favor. So what? I'm sure there are a few celebrities that you've been compared to. That doesn't make you related, does it, counselor?

"Number two, you are letting sleep deprivation mess with your mind. You owe your mother and yourself more than that. Don't let my brother's stupidity get to you."

"Ok, Marty. I'll let it go." Mia resigned feeling silly.

"Everything makes more sense when you talk it through. The more I think about it, the more ridiculous I feel for even letting it get me to this point, it was just something about the way he looked at me – like I was a prize or something . . . And then there's the fact that he mentioned my Mom by name. That just doesn't sit well. I guess that's why this has bothered me so much.

"I know it's stupid. Truly I do . . ." Then, looking at her watch, she added, "I'm gonna get back to my desk and wrap up. Mari's practice with Darren will be starting soon."

"No problem Ma'am. That's what I'm here for." Stepping around his desk to take his seat, Marty asked, "So, when are you and Darren going to make it official?"

Mia shot him an incredulous glance and rolled her eyes. "Me and Darren? Huh? What are you talking about?"

"I'm just saying. Everyone sees the way you look at each other. Don't think we miss your expressions when the other has a lunch date. I don't know what you two are waiting for." He pushed his glasses back onto the bridge of his nose and peered at Mia over the top of the frames. "I have the utmost respect for both of you and love you both like my own children. If I had any doubts, I'd tell you." He turned to his computer. "I also have the utmost confidence in your professionalism, so I know there wouldn't be any issues."

"Marty, things are fine the way they are. We're friends. I'm comfortable the way it is right now."

"Ok, it's your life. I'll tell you like I tell him all the time. No one's single forever. Don't mess around and let him get someone else under his skin, 'cause when you're finally ready, you'll be needlessly in competition with someone else. You're great friends with great chemistry and tons in common. I'm just saying..."

"Yup, gotcha," Mia cut in. "I've gotta change before heading off to practice. See you tomorrow."

"Funny, Darren does the same exact thing when I approach him with this. Have a good night . . . niece."

CHAPTER 14:
JAN 2003
In a Word – STRIDES

"CLEMSON, TEMPLE, BROWN, UCLA, and Alabama all called this week." Mari beamed. "But get this, Alabama and Clemson are also offering full academic rides!"

"That's what I'm talking about, boy. You handled your business. So, now that you've got the Big 10, SEC, ACC, and Ivy Leagues all recruiting you, where do you think you want to go?"

"Honestly, I'm between Penn State and Ohio State since they are SEC and they started hitting me up last year. Happy Valley is unbelievable and it would be amazing to play for the Lions, but I'm kinda leaning towards Ohio State. Equally huge school, great program. I'd be farther away, but close enough that I can come down for the weekend or the fam can come my way for the weekend. Y'all could even make the home games. Besides," Mari paused and rubbed his hands together slyly grinning like the cat that got the canary, "Randy and I peeped out Ohio State's cheerleaders and Oh My God..."

"Boy, don't make me come across this table," shot Elaine, half-jokingly.

"Ah Ma, come on now. You know I'm just playing."

The entire family was in town for Pittsburgh Proper's annual High School Winter Sports Banquet. Of course, Mari ran away with the offensive rushing and scoring awards. He lost the Regional Winter Sports MVP award by two points to Randall Albenschriber, his best friend for the last four years. Randy — the school quarterback's — GPA was .05 points higher than Jamari's. That was the deciding factor in a race where there were two equally qualified student athletes. Granted the MVP loss to Randy did twinge a bit, but Mari didn't dwell on it because the boys were so close. If he had to lose, there was no one else in the state to whom losing would have been even remotely acceptable.

Besides, Mari had been the man of the night. For starters, his name had been etched in history as his school's leading all-time rusher and scorer. Mari was also recognized for his selections to the All Regional and All-State Football Teams for the past three years straight. The night was capped off with the announcements of known recruitment and scholarship offers. As expected, Mari topped all other athletes in the region. He and Randy, that is. In fact, the best friends and teammates were two of the top football recruits in the Northeast.

"Now, Mari don't make any decisions based on a cheerleading uniform," quipped Bria, now twelve.

"Why not? Sounds like a good idea to me." chimed in Shamir who'd just recently crossed into the teens.

"Oh God." laughed Mia. She leaned over and whispered in Elaine's ear, "So, it's official? Girls no longer have cooties?"

"Don't get me started," Elaine half-whispered back. "Basketball has made him primetime and you can see that his body is filling out, so he's starting to feel himself. Everywhere we go, there are girls breaking their necks to ensure he sees them." She took a sip of her soda and rolled her eyes half-smiling. "Pray for your mama, baby." Elaine patted Mia's hand and turned her attention back to the handsome man of the hour.

Now seventeen, Jamari Ramon Copeland was a spitting image of his father. The only real differences were their complexions and Mari's height. Unfortunately, there was too much of Elaine in the height category. Ramon stood 6'1, while Jamari was 5'8. They had the same physique (except Mari's frame bulged with youth and athleticism). Even their strides were identical – minus the pimp that Mari had added to his swagger.

"I think you'd look good in Buckeye Red or Nittany Blue son," said Ramon. His smile and chest revealed unspeakable pride. "But then again, I think you'd look great in anything."

All eyes turned in Ramon's direction because the last few words barely eked out over the huge lump that had been steadily forming all evening in the conflicted father's throat. He had both overwhelming pride, and a nagging guilt for not being there when Mari needed him most.

"Awww, sweetheart." Elaine knowingly kissed Ramon's shoulder and hugged him all the while wiping the tear of joy that had spilled out of the corner of her own eye.

It was so great to see them together again. The reconciliation had come almost two years ago following Elaine's breast cancer diagnosis which had been found by chance following a traffic accident.

"THE AIRBAG DIDN'T deploy," Elaine said to the emergency room doctor as the EMTs wheeled her in.

Elaine recalled seeing the driver and thinking that he wasn't going to stop in time. Unfortunately, she'd been sandwiched between the white cargo van that hit her and the Honda in front of her and because she hadn't bothered to buckle up, her torso hit the steering wheel.

"My collar bone and chest hurt." That was followed by a series of yeses and no's as she replied to the ER staff's probing for additional sources of pain.

Her X-rays and CT scans were normal. She had bruised her sternum. The next ten words shifted her world slightly off its axis: "There is a spot on your breast that is concerning."

On a rainy Wednesday morning, less than a week after the accident, she was sitting in the Oncologist's office adorned with pink ribbons and riddled with positive messaging of survival. She watched as the doctor's rosy lips pursed and stretched in regular succession, but her ears had not transmitted any additional sounds to her brain after the words 'You have Stage 3 Breast Cancer' spilled from her mouth. Elaine didn't remember much about the weeks immediately following the diagnosis, but Ramon did.

He was stateside within days of getting the news. The remaining two months of his contract were left unfulfilled, and with his Amore in danger, he could not have cared less.

Initially, Ramon moved into Jamari's old room. He'd been there to care for the children and ensure that Elaine made every appointment and received round-the-clock care. Elaine being Elaine had refused all assistance from Ramon for the first week after starting chemo. So much so that when she vomited blood, she declined to mention it until her best friend, Kerry, came over five hours later. She had to stop an understandably crushed Ramon from killing Elaine.

What followed were weeks and months of treatment and rebuilding. Ramon moved back into their bedroom following Elaine's fifth round of treatment which left her too weak to ring the bell he'd gotten so that she could ask for assistance. He'd spoon fed applesauce. He'd even force-fed mashed potatoes and tamped down Elaine's apologies as he cleaned up accidents.

He'd been with her through mastectomy and radiation assuring Elaine that he hadn't married her for her breasts — regularly reminding his queen that they'd dated for years before he'd ever seen them. Ramon changed her bandages and cleaned oozing incisions. He was there to bathe her when merely stretching her arms caused searing pain. Ramon reminded Elaine daily that the scars did not define her. He'd been there offering encouragement during every tearful surveillance of her naked mutilated torso.

Ramon purchased a platinum wig and wore it every time Elaine went hair shopping. He'd playfully encourage her to try risqué colors and lengths in addition to her day-to-day hair pieces. She'd roll her eyes shaking her head in amusement at his frisky suggestions. Ramon had even been there during the subsequent breast reconstruction, earnestly recommending the HHH cups. In fact, Elaine credited her endurance and mental stability to Ramon's easy-going, humor-infused approach to life.

Throughout his constant worldwide photo-shooting adventures, Ramon yearned for Elaine's companionship. Though he'd found other women to fulfill his occasional needs, there had never been another Elaine. For that reason, Ramon ended his international aspirations. His new life's inspiration was Elaine and all the other cancer fighters he'd met during her journey.

Instead of foreign landscapes, militia, and international cultures, Ramon was dedicating his incredible talents to capturing life events and telling those stories through his lens. Elaine left her corporate position and she and Ramon now worked together in his business. She was in charge of scheduling and marketing and of course, Ramon captured the moments. They completed each other. That was obvious from their relationship, successful business, and well-adjusted, happy children — one of whom happened to be celebrating one of the biggest nights of his short life.

"Thanks, Dad," winked Mari. "Love you, man."

The family had decided that Mari would stay with Mia even after Ramon returned. After all, he'd been thriving. Mia and Mari visited every weekend during Elaine's treatments. Thereafter, they continued the biweekly visits. Mari eventually made his peace with his parents. He'd forgiven Ramon for leaving, Elaine for burying herself in her work to ease her pain, and them both for giving up on him.

Mari turned to Darren Wilford. "D, Man. I don't even know where to start..." He clasped his hand in front of his mouth and exhaled. "Yo...man...I can't thank you enough for everything. From the practice films and one-on-ones, to the fake cases you had me researching at the firm just so I could get the extra reading in, to really just being there day in and day out." He was clearly losing his battle with the tears, but Mari was putting up a valiant fight.

"All those late-night talks and early morning runs… You're the big brother that I never had. I just hope you know that I appreciate everything…" There was nothing else he could say to Darren, nothing audible was coming out. Besides, everyone already knew what he felt. Darren got up and met Mari halfway for an endearing embrace. Ramon almost missed the photo op having been caught up in that most touching moment.

"I've told you many times. I never had a little brother and I thank God for you every day. You've been as much to me as I have been to you. Believe that. I love you, boy and I'm so proud of you." Darren broke the embrace, joking that Mari was still gonna eat his dust when they went for their run in the morning. "Yeah, that's right. You don't leave until August for wherever you're going. The way I see it, you've got about eight more months of butt kickings to take."

"D, I never really thanked you for having my back when I took Goldie and hit Mr. Burress' car."

"Wait, what? Darren, I thought you told me that *you'd* hit his car because you weren't used to driving a stick shift? *You* said that *you* had to move Goldie to make space for my neighbor's moving truck and cracked his bumper after mixing up the gear shifts."

"See, Mari. There you go. I told you I wasn't gonna tell her. Now you got both of us in trouble," retorted Darren. "And I gotta work with this woman. I ain't ever gonna live this down," he joked.

Mari then turned his crooked smile towards his sister who was suppressing her smile and giving him the side eye.

"Awww come on Sis. It was a couple months after I got here and I never did it again. That was actually the day before I got saved, remember that D? We were on the practice field and I asked you if God would still love me if I messed up. Then I told you what I did?"

Darren, smiled fondly nodding his head.

"What I *didn't* know is that God was gonna tell you to make me do a hundred burpees and run two miles as punishment."

The entire table erupted in laughter.

"But seriously, Sis . . ." The words escaped him. Instead, he held his oldest sister resting his head on her soft shoulder while squeezing her tightly. Mari refused to allow himself to think of where he'd be had it not been for her love and support. By the time the embrace ended, they were both in tears.

"Thank you," Mia said to Darren as he handed her his hanky and placed his arm comfortingly around her. Mia casually leaned into him in response and her temperature instantly shot up by thirty degrees. His cologne, his essence, his voice, his breathing – Him. It was intoxicating to her. Darren placed a kiss on top of her head before somehow willing himself to release his grip. "Damn it, even her hair smells good," thought the tormented man. They each returned to their respective seats around the table — their unspoken chemistry lost on no one.

"So remind us why he's not your boyfriend," asserted Jordyn. An exasperated Mia could only roll her eyes that her precocious young sister.

"Yeah, Coach. Remind us," added Randy who'd caught the tail end of the embrace. "Our inquiring minds want to know."

"Not you too," chuckled Darren shaking his head.

That was met with a barrage of 'amens' and arguments supporting their coupling.

"I need to hit the ladies' room." When she saw that she was going to be accompanied by the family match-makers, she jokingly added, "Alone!"

CHAPTER 15:
In a word – GRADUATION

*T*HE NEXT FEW weeks were slightly awkward for Mia and Darren. They'd been cornered by her family and friends and each had an opportunity to allow themselves to dream about what a relationship could be like. Unfortunately, they were still colleagues and – for all intents and purposes – strictly off-limits. Neither of them had plans to leave WW&M so this fantasy seemed moreso a waste of time. Life continued. Cases continued. The intense lip-biting tension during elevator rides continued.

Finally, graduation arrived. Darren and Ramon took Mari shopping for a new suit. Mia and Elaine busied themselves with last-minute party preparations. As they exited their favorite Sweet Street bakery, Mia was overtaken by that eerie sense again – someone was watching her. As always, she scanned every angle looking intently for anyone/anything, but again came up empty.

"I know I'm not crazy," she whispered internally. "What is this about?"

Elaine instinctively began surveying their surroundings before asking her daughter about the source of her consternation.

"Nothing, where are we heading next?" With everything going on and her disinterest in having Elaine and Ramon move into her townhome permanently, Mia opted to dodge the topic — instead, shifting the conversation to their remaining errands.

The women returned to Mia's about an hour before they needed to leave for the ceremony. With all of the pre-graduation festivities, Mari hadn't had time to tailor their yard. As one of his gifts to Mari, Darren volunteered for the last-minute landscaping duty and was knocking that out while Ramon ran to the market for propane, charcoal and meats. They were expecting about thirty people for his party and needed enough fuel and food to keep the partygoers satisfied.

Mia shuttled helium balloons into their respective positions as she finished setting up the living room and den areas. Hearing the noise outside, she stopped briefly to survey the outdoor progress. What she found was Darren in a blue fitted tank deftly willing the long green blades into submission. She allowed herself to peruse his own personal landscaping. His powerful muscles cloaked by a smooth cocoa caramel complexion. Perspiration glistened from his scalp before streaking across the hills and valleys of his physique before disappearing into the shirts' ever-darkening shades of blue. "Good God!"

She'd seen him sweaty and active multiple times throughout the years, but she'd never been able to fully appreciate the view without fear of someone catching her mid-stare.

Having completed the yard, Darren snuck off to Mari's room to shower and change, something he'd done from time to time during the years. This time, he found Mari's room occupied by the girls. With time quickly dwindling, he'd have to use Mia's. Darren had seen her room as part of the obligatory tour that most people give upon guests first time at their home.

He'd never actually seen the upstairs since that moment a few years back. Darren and Mia met as he was ascending the stairs and she was exiting her room. The air caught in her throat as the now shirtless specimen cleared the final two steps up to the landing. The heat from the sun and his exertions still radiated off his body.

Mia swallowed as her trembling fingers plucked a blade of grass that had gotten stuck to his sweaty bicep.

"There's a rag and towel on the sink for you and I put –."

Her words were cut short by his sudden, unexpected kiss. Before she knew it, her arms were locked around his damp neck. Their tongues longingly intertwining. Years of pent up desire coursed through their beings. Darren's hands skillfully, simultaneously caressing her face and lower back while Mia's hands cradled the curves of his sexy scalp. His body pressed against hers. She groaned softly in response while her hand traced the strong contours of his jaw.

"Mia? Mia where are you? Mom wants you," yelled Bria.

They reluctantly returned to reality. Darren bit his lip as he watched her descent. She looked back in his direction before turning the corner to find her mom on the patio.

Darren crossed Mia's room heading towards the shower, envying the green chenille covers and their ability to wrap around her each night. Her walk-in closet wasn't overflowing with unnecessary clothing and she had an ample amount of open space. Man, he'd love to hang a few shirts in there.

"God, could you please make a way?"

———————⁓———————

"IT'S THE DAMNEDEST thing. I must have picked up a nail," mused Ramon as he studied the flat rear tire on his Suburban. Shamir noticed it as everyone was filing out heading to the ceremony. The plan was to have everyone ride together in Ramon's vehicle, but with the unexpected flat, the family piled into Darren's Escalade. While the Copelads and Darren all viewed this as an unfortunate incident, Mia couldn't help but wonder if there was something more to it. She scolded herself for even considering the possibility. Afterall, why would anyone intentionally flatten her dad's tire?

CHAPTER 16:
In a Word – REALIZATIONS

*O*N JULY 4, 2003, Darren's dreams finally came true. It was the day that he'd found the courage to ask Mia out and it was the same day that she said yes. Fortunately, it was not too long after having shared that brief, passionate kiss at the top of her stairs. That encounter left the normally laser-focused Defense Attorney hopelessly distracted for weeks.

Still thinking that they could never be a true couple, Mia and Darren attended a city-wide evening concert and BBQ on the river hosted by WAMO radio – both had shown up with their respective dates. It wasn't until Mia saw Darren clinging bottles and hamming it up with his gorgeous partner, that she'd completely understood Marty's earlier advice. At that moment, she accepted that her feelings for Darren were way beyond friendship. Amia Copeland adored that man and had no interest in seeing him romantically involved with anyone else.

She took the first chance she got to speak to Darren alone. She pulled him into the makeshift dance floor and they stayed there for four straight songs. By the third song, each of Mia's hands held a red heeled sandal while the beads of sweat forming on Darren's forehead started trickling down the sides of his face. Before she knew it, Mia had gently dabbed a few beads and was cradling his face with her hands. Thankfully, the fourth song had been a slow jam. Darren's unrelenting fantasy of holding Mia close again was actually happening and he knew he had to act to move their relationship to the next level.

"It's now or never, Darren."

He leaned his head closer so that his lips brushed against Mia's earlobe and said just above the blaring music, "I'm dropping her off after the fireworks. Can we get something to eat afterwards?"

Electricity shot from her earlobe down to her feet leaving goosebumps in its wake. "I don't want either of us to be on the road tonight because everyone's drinking and it's not safe..." Mia inhaled his masculinity and added, "You want to work out with me and have breakfast in the morning?" From that moment on, the two had been an item. They'd kept the relationship hidden from their co-workers and Jamari for almost a year which turned out to be a smart decision because the union was almost over before it really took off.

October 2003

"WAIT, YOU'RE SAYING that we should do what?"

"I'm saying that we need to break up. We need some time apart.

"Babe, slow down. We're not breaking up."

"This is exactly what I wanted to avoid, Darren. Now look at us. I don't want to either, but I can't do this," she exclaimed as she tucked her breasts back into her bra.

"We need a break. Clearly, we've gotten out of order. I'm so ashamed of myself," she said averting her eyes from her reflection in the large adjacent wall mirror.

"I know," he said, having slipped his khakis back on.

"All I want to do is hide my face from God," she added burying her head in her hands.

"I don't even want to go to church tomorrow. How can I . . . I'm a fraud. How do I go into church pretending like I'm all good and upstanding and all the while, I'm acting like . . . like . . . this," she said flinging her arms.

Darren sat silently on the edge of the bed. The same one that would have supported the two lovers had their beautiful bodies completely succumbed to their passions. Darren pulled his striped polo back on looking away as Mia retrieved her flowered blouse from his strong outstretched hand. After confirming that she was again fully dressed, he led her into her kitchen.

"First of all Mia, *our* God would never tell you that you can't show your face in *His* church. *Our* God can't wait to see you at the altar. You know that. You are a virtuous woman. You are fearfully and wonderfully made. Don't you ever question that. You know who's trying to sell you those lies."

"I know," she replied. "But we've gotta figure something out. I'm not going to Hell because we can't keep our hands off of each other. What happens the next time, Darren? What if we can't stop ourselves? I don't want that for either of us."

Darren planted himself on one of the wrought iron ivory island stools and motioned Mia to sit beside him.

"I know and I hear you Babe. But breaking up, separating, taking a break — all of those options are completely off the table," Darren said. Then, resting his elbow on the island and leaning towards the woman of his dreams, "So, what's your other offer," he asked moving the discussion towards a peaceful negotiation.

After pondering for a few moments, "What if we start seeing each other only once a week?"

"Nope."

"You can't just decline without a counteroffer, Counselor," Mia smiled.

"What else you got?"

"We can see each other, but never at each other's homes."

"That's called avoidance. Nope. We've gotta be able to hang out together at our homes. What else you got?"

"Darren, Mia exclaimed with phony exasperation."

"Mia. I've rejected each of your last two offers," he replied smiling while stroking his goatee. "What else you got?"

"I'll be back."

Mia returned to the small kitchen thirty minutes later with two pieces of paper.

"Really, a contract Babe?"

"Uh-huh. Read it." she smiled from the opposite side of the island; eyes completely focused on her handsome counterpart.

" . . . the two aforementioned parties hereby agree to keep kissing to a five-second maximum. The two aforementioned parties agree to keep hugging to a ten-second maximum. The parties further agree that the other party's breasts, genitalia, gluteus maximus and pectoral regions are exempt from intentional touch, discussion, or other activity that may cause undue attention. The aforementioned parties agree that there shall be no lustful or sexual activity until such time that the parties are married. Failure to comply with the terms of this agreement shall result in dissolution of the romantic courtship between Darren R. Wilford and Amia J. Copeland."

"You really want us to sign a contract, Ms. Copeland?"

"Uh-huh," she nodded. "And would you prefer to do so in blue or black ink, Mr. Wilford?"

Joy returned to the atmosphere as the pair happily signed both copies. Once each had been sealed in individual envelopes, Darren asked Mia to again have a seat next to him at the island.

"The bible says he who finds a wife, finds a good thing. You're not my wife yet, but you *are* my good thing. God made you for me. Of that, I'm sure. Amia Copeland, there ain't no way I'm going to let foolishness ruin my good thing . . . This right here. You and me. This is God's will.

"I have wanted you by my side ever since that Tuesday when you strolled into the main conference room and began ripping ADA Berry's case against Mark Warner to shreds."

"Really? The Mark Warner case was around my fourth month at WW&M."

"You don't have to tell me how long it's been. We were all heading to the Pirates game right after that meeting. I remember you owning every inch of that Pirates jersey," he reminisced.

"Listen Mia, I want you. God knows I do, but that can wait. I appreciate the contract but I don't need it," he paused and painfully exhaled before continuing.

"I saw my life flash before my eyes when you left the kitchen a while ago. I want to spend the rest of my days with you, loving every inch of you, but I will honor us both and above all, I will honor God. I swear I won't ever put either of us in this position again."

"Darren, you weren't alone back there in that room. I'm just as much to blame for − ."

"No Mia. This is on me," he paused to rub his temples.

"I'm supposed to be the head. My family does as I do. Baby, I never want to cause you to want to hide from God," he added. His chest literally ached at the thought. "God has blessed this. He wants us to be together and we will honor Him."

"MEETING IN AC4. I know that's what the invite said," Mia mused as she exited the empty second-floor conference room. She hurried back to her desk to recheck the email, unable to ask any of her colleagues as it was an all-staff meeting and presumably everyone was already in the correct room.

"AC4. What in the world?" she wondered after rereading the email. The entire office was a ghost town. Upon her return to AC4, she passed several offices looking into the vacant spaces hoping to find at least one person.

"I don't understand, AC4 is empty. Was there another email changing the room?" Mia fussed at herself for not thinking of that before heading back down to the second floor for the second time. Back at her desk, sure enough. There was another email. Today's meeting would be in the atrium.

"Yes!" Mia exclaimed. Meetings in the atrium were always informal and included pizza.

The elevator dinged announcing her arrival to the first floor. She screamed as she found the love of her life on one knee next to WW&M's famous four-tiered fountain. The sunlight kissed a beautiful three-carat diamond ring causing prisms to twinkle across Darren's black button down. The WW&M staff lined the walls, each holding a red rose. Gary and Mable and Ramon and Elaine were positioned on either side of the marbled centerpiece.

"You're always early to our meetings, so I had to get creative," smiled Darren.

"I would have done this last week, but as you know, mom and dad over there," playfully tilting his head and rolling his eyes towards Gary and Mable before continuing, "Were out of the country. They got back yesterday and drove into Pittsburgh this morning."

"Mia blew a kiss to Gary and Mable and mouthed "Thank you" as she wiped her cascading tears.

"Amia Copeland —".

"Yes, Darren. I will!"

"Wait Baby, I haven't asked you yet."

"I don't care. Yes!"

"Hold up, Amia," Darren said while laughing and holding her shaking hand. "I've spent the last few years rehearsing this in my mind. Let me get it out."

Mia's happy, restless feet aptly represented the joy emanating through her being. She didn't need him to say how he felt. God showed her his heart. Every molecule, every eyelash, every fiber in his being loved her — and she felt it.

"Amia, you are my heart's desire," he began.

"You are my air. You're the answer to every one of my prayers. My best friend and my soulmate. You are the one who God designed just for me. I know this because you check all the boxes — even the ones I hadn't thought of."

Darren paused to compose himself, using his red pocket handkerchief to dab the tears that began streaming as soon as the elevator doors opened.

"You make me a better man. My heart sings your song. You are my good thing. Every day is brighter and sweeter because you grace it. Sweetheart, you make me happier than I ever imagined possible. I want to grow old with you. I want to climb mountains and take in God's beauty with you. The only one I want in the valley with me, is you. Babe, I want to experience going grey and counting wrinkles with you.

Amia Jasmine Copeland, I love you. Would you please do me the honor of being my wife?"

The two boxes of Kleenex had been emptied by the time Mia officially said yes – partially because the staff had been secretly rooting for this union for years. The other reason is because they'd successfully pulled off this secret proposal. Darren made Marty, Geoff, and Mike aware of his intentions the Monday immediately following his and Mia's encounter at her place. Because WW&M was an extended family for them both, Darren asked everyone to join him in the atrium that afternoon.

Rhonda Horne began an impromptu serenade of the couple as Matt continued playing his keyboard. He'd offered to add his gift to the moment after receiving Darren's email earlier in the week and had been continuously stroking the keys since ten minutes prior to their 'meeting'.

CHAPTER 17:
In a Word – UNEXPECTED

T HE WILFORD-COPELAND WEDDING in October 2004 followed their year-long engagement and was the talk of the town. As an inspiring and now prominent African American couple, they were featured on BET and in Essence and Ebony Magazines. The city's district attorneys, prosecutors, judges, politicians, university officials, and the like all offered their congratulations and best wishes. Even Oprah had congratulated them on their nuptials. Yes, that Oprah!

Though they'd spent thousands on their wedding, tens of thousands more were saved due to generous gifts from anonymous donors. As justice officials, it wasn't possible for them to knowingly accept expensive gifts, so Marty, Geoff, and Mike created a separate account for wedding donations and appointed a trustee to oversee the disbursement of funds. The sheer brilliance of the firm's attorneys was awe-inspiring at times. After all, they'd known that anonymous donations offered a welcome circumvention to the long-standing anti-lobbying legislation.

About a year later after the nuptials, Mia was having lunch with Elaine at one of their favorite Chinese restaurants.

"Eww, this fried rice is nasty. It smells weird and tastes like grease. Is your rice ok," she asked pushing her plate away, her face distorted in disgust.

"Yeah, my rice is fine. Tastes like it always does."

"No, something's weird. . . Excuse me, waitress. I don't know what it is, but this rice tastes bad. Can I get Lo Mein instead?"

The waitress hurried away with the rice returning a few minutes later with Mia's pasta.

"This is much better. Thank you." And with that, Mia continued her meal.

"Are you pregnant, Mia?"

"What? No, Ma. I'm not pregnant. The rice was nasty. What are you talking about?"

"I'm just saying, it tastes fine to me and I'm sure they both came out of the same pot, but what do I know," Elaine smiled and sipped her tea.

"Really, the pinky finger? Really Mom?"

That pinky finger was Elaine's sign that something was amiss. She'd shown it while sipping coffee when Mia was a sixth grader desperately denying that Sam Johnson had a crush on her. She'd extended it in high school when Mia had a crush on the star basketball player but refuted Elaine's accusation, and she'd sipped her Pepsi out of a straw with her pinky extended to the sky the night of Mari's graduation when Mia rested her head on Darren's chest.

"Mom. Stop. Flo just left two weeks ago. She was on time and normal," Mia recalled of her monthly visitor.

The next morning, she sat smiling in disbelief while staring at the double blue lines. She had picked up the test on the way home from lunch with Elaine. Mia and Darren hadn't planned to get pregnant so quickly, but she was ecstatic. Her next thought was to pinpoint when she got pregnant, but they were still newlyweds – so that was impossible. Although, there was that one time on the balcony a few weeks ago . . .

"Go get it. Go get your toys," urged Darren to the never-ending balls of energy called Sugar and Ray. The pups were now three-years-old and showed zero signs of shedding the puppy vitality – though the breeder assured him that they would have calmed down by now.

"Sugar, get your toy."

Instead of returning with the tug toy, the white Boxer began sprinting across the floor chasing an elusive FedEx box with her nose. Darren watched amused while the rambunctious pup barked at the box as if ordering it to stop moving. When the barking failed to gain compliance, she pawed the cardboard jumping backwards as it flipped in response to the pressure. Darren decided to intervene before the contents got destroyed.

A box inside of a box. Another box inside of that box . . . A third box wrapped in newspaper. "What is going on here?"

"Who's it from, babe?" asked Mia curiously.

"I don't know. It's one box after the other and now there's this box covered in newspaper."

Darren unraveled the newspaper to find a long black jewelry box with a note that read simply, "For the Man I love."

"Babe, you got me the bracelet? You're too much," he smiled while planting a juicy kiss on her full lips.

"Open it," she urged nudging him softly.

Mia hadn't considered, prior to tucking the wand inside the jewelry box and stuffing it into the subsequent packages, that Darren had no idea what a pregnancy test stick looked like – let alone what the two blue lines meant. His confusion was clearly evident.

"Babe, what is it?" he asked extracting the utensil and casually flipping it.

"It's a test."

"Okayyy, is there a hint," he asked.

"Babe, it's a test, she laughed."

"What kind of test?" Darren mused again flipping the plastic form before attempting to remove its cap.

Mia quickly grabbed his hand. "You don't wanna do that."

Darren paused to study his wife's humorous facial

expressions. Though this announcement wasn't going at all as she'd planned, it was perfect. Mia was already imagining herself retelling this story for decades to come.

"What is so funny, babe? What am I missing here? There's a stick with two blue lines and I shouldn't remove the lid."

Two seconds later, it clicked. Darren realized that he was holding Mia's pregnancy test.

"Are you . . . Oh my God," he cried as she nodded emphatically.

CHAPTER 18:
In a Word – CORRIDORS

"*H*URRY BACK, THEY'LL be starting soon," Elaine said to the Bria and Jordyn as they hustled off to the restroom. She wanted to ensure the girls were back before the Mayor took the stage.

"Our honorees of the hour, Jamari Ramon Copeland and Randall Albenschiber are being recognized for their selflessness and fearlessness for running into a burning building to rescue three women and two children who'd been trapped in a second-floor apartment." The mayor continued, "By now, you know the story. While home from their respective universities for the winter break, these two young men – Prides of Pittsburgh – happened to get lost while on the Northside. A light turns yellow and for some reason, this time, rather than flooring it," he paused to chuckle with the crowd, "Randall decided to stop. Turns out to have been a fateful decision because within seconds, both young men were charging into the burning complex banging on doors and alerting other unassuming tenants of the inferno. They were able to kick the door in and guide the trapped family to safety..."

The Mayor's speech was followed by a few other distinguished attendees as well as representatives from their respective universities who were there to celebrate Randy and Jamari's achievements.

"I'm proud of you, Man," exclaimed a proud Ramon.

"This is crazy!" exclaimed Mari after returning to the table, Key to the City in tow. "I honestly never expected any of this. We jumped out of the car and were in the building before we even had a chance to think. I'm just glad we were there."

"That's what's up! I'm proud of you man! But I have a question. . . Do I have to call you 'Sir' now," joked Darren.

"If so, are you ready to eat dust in the morning, Sir? Now that school's out, you've got a few more months of butt kickings to take before you go back in August."

That's where you're wrong," added Elaine. "*The way I see it*, you've got a few months until this baby gets here and then you'll be too tired to kick his butt in the mornings."

"Oooh, how right you are," laughed Darren walking back over to kiss Mia's cheek and pat her growing belly.

"Speaking of the baby, I need to hit the restroom again," added an absolutely radiant Mia. Pregnancy was agreeing with her. This night, her there-but-barely bump was peeking out of a baby blue cashmere sweater paired with brown maternity trousers. She finished the outfit with a cute pair of two-inch boots, which would be retired immediately upon their arrival at home that evening.

"I'll go with you," said Elaine grabbing her purse. "Anyone else need to go?" That question was directed at Jordyn and Bria and received an almost immediate, simultaneous "nooooo." They were uber independent nowadays and wanted no parts of public family bathroom visits.

"Bring my wife back in one piece," joked Darren. As the women headed off to the bathroom, Darren commented on how quickly the years had gone. "It's hard to believe it's been two years already."

"You think you're peeing now, wait 'til you're eight and nine months. You ain't seen nothing yet. Just go ahead and ask Darren to blow up an air mattress in the bathroom because that's where you'll be most of the time." Elaine hugged her oldest daughter. It was hard to believe that Mia was now thirty-three. It seemed like yesterday that she'd gone off to prom and then college. Now, she's happily married and carrying her own baby.

After checking their makeup and hair, the ladies headed down the long, cream tile and carpeted corridor leading back into the auditorium. Mia stopped to admire a few of the paintings that she'd seen on the way to the restroom but had been in too much of a hurry to peruse. Since being with Darren, Mia had developed an appreciation for all things designer. She was interested in the colors, textures, balance, and textiles that all contributed to the look and feel of a room. Before Darren, there was no way she'd have ever stopped to admire paintings. Truth be told, she'd never taken a moment to notice anything other than the people in any given place.

As she marveled at the artist's stampeding pack of mustangs brought to life with dabs of brown and streaks of white, Mia became acutely aware of another presence in the hallway. Elaine had been fumbling through her purse for a mint while Mia unraveled the mystery of a second painting. Both women unceremoniously stepped backward letting the passerby through.

Mia offered a polite "excuse us" while trying not to inhale too deeply as the aroma increasingly transitioned from fresh and crisp to loud, stale cigarettes and cheap, pungent alcohol.

"No, excuse me, baby girl," an eerily familiar tone bellowed. "Damn, I'm good. My baby is fine."

That unique, throaty voice stole Elaine's attention away from her intense perusal. Her entire being transfixed in disbelief, so much so that she'd dropped her purse, but hadn't seemed to hear it hit the ground or spill its contents. Following her conversations with Marty and Darren years earlier, Amia hadn't really given Maxwell's comments any more thought, but now she knew that there was something that she'd been in the dark about all these years.

Mia collected the strewn belongings and offered them to the Copeland matriarch. "Mom? Here's your purse." Elaine's body seemed to have shut down due to the shock of seeing what can only be described as a present-day ghost. Mia linked her arm with Elaine's unresponsive form firmly coaxing her body into motion. A split second later, she snapped out of it glaring at Maxwell and pushing past him holding tightly onto Mia's arm.

"So, I guess it is true, huh? Looks like I'm gonna be a granddad. You didn't even invite your old pops to your wedding, but that's cool. I saw the pictures."

"What the Hell are you doing here?" asked Elaine angrily through her clenched teeth.

"You not happy to see me again? That hurts. I'm really just here to see my baby girl."

"You are not her father. Ramon is. Remember him? Ramon is Amia's father and he will be right back to holla at you."

"It's all good 'Lanie. You're still as fine as I remember. You got a little thicker in the thighs and hips, but I like that."

"Go to Hell!" Elaine spat.

"Still fiery, too. Damn. You know, I still think about all that passion we shared back then and those lips, Lanie." Max feigned a shiver and leered at her longingly. He then redirected his attention to Mia. "No way I'mma miss the birth of my only grandchild."

"She is not your child, but you know what, I can show you better than I can tell you." She pulled her stunned daughter into the breezeway.

They were just outside of the reserved banquet

room when Mia asked, "What just happened? Mom, how do you know him?"

"Mia, please trust me. I will explain everything, but this is Mari's night. We will talk, but I can't right now."

"Mom, I can't just act like that didn't happen. Did you know Marty before I introduced you? Does everyone know but me and..." fear crept over Mia's face. "Dad? Does Dad know? Were you really going to send him back to deal with Maxwell?" Mia scratched her head. "Mom? Answer me. What's going on?"

"Amia, I can't do this. Please know there's nothing to tell. Ramon is your father. There was nothing between Maxwell and –."

"Awww, Lanie. We both know that's not true, don't we?" Maxwell countered, calmly sliding into the foyer with the women before strolling out of the sprawling conference center.

Mia winced at a twinge in her lower belly. "Mom," Mia whispered now horrified, "I don't know if I really want to know –."

"Amia, I love you. That's all you need to know. Ramon Copeland is your father."

Confused and half in shock, Mia leaned against the blue and white paisley wall-papered hallway and watched in disbelief as Maxwell blew a kiss and pushed through the glass roundabout disappearing into the night. She gathered her strength and looked back at her mother whose incredulous gaze had become fixated on one of the hundreds of blue diamonds woven into the corridor's beige carpeting.

"That is the second time he's said that to me. Mom. Mom?" Mia sternly whispered. Mia grabbed her mom's arms to get her attention. "Mom, listen to me. I need to know what's going on here."

Elaine gasped angrily after learning that Maxwell had approached her daughter before. "When?" Elaine whispered, trying to keep her voice down through her mounting anger.

"A couple of years ago at Hershey."

"Why didn't you say anything to me then?"

"Because I talked to Marty and Darren who reminded me that Maxwell was a dribbling drunk and not to waste my time on him. I didn't bring it to you honestly because it didn't make any sense. I just decided to let it go."

Just then, the door opened as the father-to-be came in search of his wife and mother-in-law. Noticing the tension in the air, he closed the door behind him and stepped into the awkwardly silent hallway. "Hey, baby... Elaine? What's wrong?" The duo stood there silently for a few moments until Elaine's fire came to a head.

"I'm 'bout to do what I should have done years ago. I'mma kill his sorry ass," she spat through clenched, seething lips. "Mia, you won't have to worry about Maxwell Worthy popping up anymore."

"Max?" Darren uttered trying to wrap his head around the atmosphere and Elaine's anger. "What does he have to do with...Wait, he's here? What did he say? Where is he?" Darren rushed into the atrium and returned promptly after not seeing him. "Did he hurt you? Mia?"

"No. He congratulated himself on becoming a granddad," she hissed.

"That is straight bullshit!" Elaine's eyes glared and fist clenched. "But it's all good..."

"Elaine. Calm down. We'll take care of this. Is he still here?" Darren asked.

"No," Mia answered. "He left about three minutes ago." She paused remembering the occasion. "This is Mari's big night. Let's forget about Maxw, er, him. Under no circumstances will he ruin this incredible evening. Let's get back in there." Mia tilted her head towards the banquet room. "We'll talk in the morning."

"He'll be dead in the morning."

"Mom!"

"Mrs. Copeland!" Mia and Darren exclaimed simultaneously. Both shot worried expressions.

Before they could say anything more, she opened the banquet door, flashed her biggest smile, and returned to the table apologizing to the family members for being away for so long. She advised that they'd gotten caught up while examining the paintings in the hallway outside their door.

CHAPTER 19:
In a Word – DARREN

THE NEXT THREE days were a blur. The Pittsburgh air, sun, and sky all felt differently now that it was clear there was something to the drunken rantings of Maxwell Worthy.

"Still no answer." She exhaled with frustration throwing her cell phone down next to her on their gray microfiber sectional sofa where she'd spent most of her time since Friday evening's encounter. She and Darren left slightly before the end of Mari's night as Mia began feeling tension in her lower belly. After a quick check up at UPMC, she was assured that her baby and pregnancy were fine.

Still, as a precaution, she was placed on bed rest for a week and ordered to eliminate stress which was proving to be especially difficult since Elaine and Ramon had essentially gone dark since the awards night. They were supposed to have stayed in Pittsburgh for another night so that Elaine and Mia could talk. Instead, they headed back to Lancaster.

Mia knew that her parents were alive and well as she had been able to speak with Shamir and the girls frequently. Adding to her frustration, neither Elaine nor Ramon would answer or speak when requested. From the background, they would simply advise that they loved her and would call her back.

"This is ridiculous. We need to get to Lancaster now."

"Babe, you can't go anywhere right now. You know that. I don't know what's happening or what they're thinking, but we'll figure it out." While he wouldn't fully verbalize his frustration with Mia's parents, he was much angrier than he'd let on to his wife. The pair had always been able to share their deepest thoughts, but there was no way he'd go there with Mia in her current condition. Instead, he picked up the tug toys and began playing with Sugar and Ray.

"And what about Marty, Darren? What does he know? Why is his brother saying that he's my father? I just can't believe that he doesn't know anything about it?" She buried her head in both hands and massaged her throbbing temples.

Darren tossed both tug toys and eased down next to her scooping her bent knees and laying them across his lap. "We'll figure it out," he repeated. "You know, Marty. He's a man of God. He's real. He's the most honorable and amazing man we know. We just need to talk to him."

Leaning his head back against the couch and eyeing

one of several large, white beams spanning the ceiling of their two-story industrial condo, he said, "Honestly, honey, I don't care if you're Fidel Castro's biological child." He turned her face gently with his hand and met her uncertain eyes with calming reassurance. "It doesn't change anything for me. I love you. I'm in love with you. 'Til death do us part, remember?" He grabbed her hand, gently kissing her palm. "I'm your husband and I'm not going anywhere, Amia Copeland Wilford."

Speaking at just above a whisper, "Elaine and Ramon do need to come off it and answer some questions, though." While his irritation was well contained — evident only by his slightly flared nostrils — Mia recognized the anger in her husband's elongated exhales. She'd seen it after he received last-minute motions or summons from prosecutors and other attorneys or learned of intentional omissions by clients. Generally, it's followed by Darren interlocking his fingers behind his head and studying the ceiling.

Her eyes scanned his silhouette from his hair-covered chest to his collar bone to his Adam's apple, across his healthy lips, nose, eyelids, and to his ever-so-slightly receding hairline. Mia was reminded why she loved this incredible man so deeply.

He was everything she'd asked God for. Darren's sex appeal was enhanced exponentially by his confidence and strength, his character and integrity, and his deliciously sculpted physique. His humor, friendship, and smile were the icing on the cake of her well-dressed and impeccably groomed husband's package. Jesus, she loved that man. Mia found herself biting her lower lip as she was reminded of a Saturday afternoon not too long ago when they'd broken in the springs of their most comfortable piece of living room furniture. Mia inhaled allowing Addie's fragrant Mango Papaya creation fill her nostrils.

"What?" Darren asked curiously, raising his head from his intertwined fingers and turning towards Mia. "Why you lookin' at me like that?" He inhaled sharply as Mia quickly shifted, straddling him. She threw the tug toys to the other side of the home and instructed the pups to stay there. "Umm, Mrs. Wilford. What are you doing, sweetheart? You...umm...know...ummm... that you're...on bed rest." He managed between impassioned kisses.

"Some parts of me are, Mr. Wilford. Others... ummm... are... not." She smiled at him wryly and began leaving a hot trail of alternating kisses and long, deliberate licks down the center of her wonderfully amazing husband's beautiful body. As always, she was rewarded by his raw, wanton gasping as she engulfed him – his fingers tangling repeatedly and almost desperately in her hair.

CHAPTER 20:
In a Word – NIGHTMARE

MIA STRETCHED LAZILY, reluctantly pushing off the comfortable twenty-year-old quilted blanket. She'd fallen in love with its feel during a weekend stay at Gary and Mable's cottage almost two years ago. Mia had raved about it so much that Mable gave the quilt to her as a wedding gift. To help her endure Darren's incredibly difficult legal period, she'd stitched the blue and white treasure while in the courtroom listening to his and everyone else's testimony during Darren's father's trial.

Whenever Mia needed a deep sleep, that blanket did the trick. She had become so fond of the thatched quilt that over the past year, it had become her constant late-night movie and travel companion.

Mia freshened up, grabbed one of Darren's old oversized T-shirts, and strolled into the kitchen to find her man hard at work. There was a delicious tomato sauce simmering and he was intently reading the instructions on the box of spaghetti sticks.

"Just let them boil for eleven minutes," she said recalling the number of times she'd heard Elaine say the same thing to her.

"Hey, baby. How'd you sleep?"

"That blanket did me in again," she replied, quickly kissing his cheek. "It's 5:49? Really?" She asked, after noticing the time on their stainless-steel stove. "Babe, you should have woken me up."

"No Ma'am. Both my babies needed their rest. Especially, you. You haven't slept much lately. And besides, Mrs. Wilford..." He leaned in playfully nibbling on her freshly spritzed neck while reminiscing about her impassioned oral love making just a few hours earlier. "You earned every bit of that nap. Had me in here screaming like a little . . ."

Mia smiled at her husband slyly, playfully teasing him about his toes curling. The pair continued their impish banter while awaiting the stove's timer.

The dogs began feverishly whining and yelping at the front door just as the couple finished dinner. It wasn't the normal "someone's here" barking. It was different and higher pitched. Darren and Mia uneasily studied their fur babies' behavior as the pups focused their energies squarely at the black rectangular barrier. They hadn't heard this bellowing or seen this level of distress before. A few seconds later, there was a knock at the door. While the barks became more familiar, there was still an underlying, concerning tone. Darren commanded Sugar and Ray to stay while shooing Mia into the protection of the adjoining room. Cautiously, Darren answered the door.

"Hi, Coach. Is Jamari here?" It was Randy. His voice was trembling and he was clearly shaken.

"Randy? Come in. No, he's not here. What's wrong? What's? What's going on?"

Mia rushed over as his knees buckled, escaping serious head injury as Darren caught him as his head scraped the tile floor. He dragged Randy inside and asked Mia to get him some water. Upon her return, she noticed blood on Darren's Temple U T-shirt.

"Darren, he's bleeding!"

Only then did Darren notice the deep splotches on his favorite tank. He instructed Mia to get some towels. "Randy, what happened? Who did this? Where were you?"

At the same time, Darren could hear Mia confirming their address with 9-1-1. "I don't know, he's bleeding. Randall Albenschriber.... twenty... My husband has blood all over his shirt!"

Darren had gone into coach and trainer mode, instantly pulling at Randy's black tee and his short frantically searching for the sources of blood. He found two stab wounds in Randy's pale abdomen and one above his right hip. While there was ample bleeding, Darren did not feel that the injuries were life-threatening.

"A tall, skinny older guy came to the court where

we were running ball. He got in the game and started talking trash. Next thing I knew, he and Mari were exchanging blows."

"Mari was fighting the man? Why? What did he look like? What'd he say?" The husband/wife team fired off question after question. While Mia stayed on the line with the dispatcher, she was only half-listening once Darren advised that he thought Randy would be fine.

"I pulled Mari away and told him to squash it 'cause he wasn't worth it. The guy just laughed and left. I asked Mari what happened and he said that the man said something disrespectful about Ms. Elaine."

"Did he say what?" Darren rushed this question as the emergency sirens had graduated from faint to blaring. They could hear the rescuers noisily ascending the stairs. Mia went to open the door. She was stopped dead in her tracks by Randy's next words . . .

"He said that all he needed was another minute and Mia would have been a twin."

Dumbfounded, Mia sunk against the hallway wall displacing the 16 x 20 wedding photo of the bride, groom, and both sets of parents. Tears welled as she steadied their prized portrait which captured the happiest day of her life. Angst arrived as her fingers touched Elaine and Ramon's faces.

The EMTs advised that the wounds appeared to be caused by a short, sharp blade. Their initial assessment confirmed Darren's findings. Randy appeared to have been spared internal injuries, but he would get x-rays to confirm. Hearing this, the police began interrogating Randy asking for a description of his attacker as he was wheeled out to the ambulance. Randy told the officers that Mari was so angry that he decided to walk. He added that he'd been attacked at his car when he popped the trunk to toss his basketball in. The attacker had come up behind him, covered his mouth, and stabbed him repeatedly. He explained that he elbowed the man, scrambled into his car, and sped off searching for Jamari which is why he ended up at the Wilford's.

With all the commotion, Mia almost missed their ringing phone. An officer near the kitchen motioned to the phone's location.

"Mari?" she asked desperately.

"Hey, sweetheart," the voice on the other end stated arrogantly. "It's your daddy. You know, you really shouldn't wear his clothes. You look so much better in your own."

"How'd you get my num - ? Where is my brother?"

"Your half-brother. Get that shit right," he spat. "That negro obviously don't know his place. You better school his ass, baby girl. Let him or anyone else step to me like that again, they'll get more than a couple of paper cuts."

Mia grabbed the lead investigator and Darren after Max revealed that he was close enough to see her.

"Keep him on the line," mouthed the lead investigator.

The APB was put out from the lead investigator who had set up shop in Mari's room. "All Units, be advised. Suspect is a Black Male about 6'5" 200 pounds. He is wearing a grey sweatshirt and black pants. He should be considered armed and dangerous." They meshed Mia's description of Max with Randy's description of the clothing..

"Maxwell, what do you want?"

In a surprisingly earnest tone, he continued.

"I just want you to know your real pops. Do you know how many years I've had to sit by and watch Ramon get all the credit for my work? And Marty acting like I don't exist. The first time I saw you was five years ago at the law firm. You were there with your mother. I'll never forget it. You looked right through me as if I wasn't there. But I knew instantly that you were mine."

Mia listened in sickened disbelief as Max continued. A call was coming in on her other line, but the officers insisted that she ignore it. Apprehending Max was their top priority.

"Have you been following me?"

"Following you? Come on, baby girl. I'm your Daddy. I've been keeping an eye on you these past few years. Just been waiting on the right time to tell you.

"Check this out. I know you get your groceries on 5th and that you like lemon slices in your sprite. I know you grab coffee at Jack's and you like ranch on your spaghetti. You park on the 4th floor of the parking garage across from the courthouse. I've even let you pass me a few times on the running path off of Dearborne. Yeah, I've been watching you ever since –"

"Freeze! Put your hands up and step away from the

bushes — now!" So grateful to hear those words, she dropped the cordless phone and hugged Darren tightly.

Though he'd only been spewing his filth in Mia's ear for a few minutes before being apprehended, it seemed like hours.

Just then, Darren's phone rang.

"Hello, this is Margaret from Allegheny General Emergency Department. Jamari Copeland listed you as one of his emergency contacts."

"Yes, how is he?" asked Darren almost afraid to hear the answer but praying for good news.

"I can't release details on his condition, but I can tell you that we will be taking him back for emergency surgery shortly.

Immediately, the couple advised the officers that they would be heading to the hospital.

CHAPTER 21:
In a Word – SPARED

"**H**OW DO YOU plead?" Judge Rendita bellowed from behind the huge 100-year-old cherrywood desk. "Mr. Worthy? I will not ask you again."

Max winked at Mia, Darren, Elaine, and Ramon sitting caddie corner on the prosecution's side of the court room. He then stood straight, looked Judge Rendita in his eyes, and declared proudly, "Not guilty, your Honor."

Charged with two counts of aggravated assault, two counts of assault with a dangerous weapon, second-degree stalking, and terroristic threats for threatening to blow up Mari's dorm and the Copeland' home, Max was remanded without bail pending trial.

Though never one to play politics, Marty called in a favor to the district attorney, specifically requesting that The People relay the gravity of the crimes and hit him with every available charge in the book. He reminded his counterparts that both youngsters had recently been given the Keys to the City and had been making the rounds as City Ambassadors. Marty's goal was to ensure Max would not be released on bail. They'd been fielding requests from media and had been hounded by paparazzi ever since the prior Monday. Rumors were starting to swirl about Jamari and Max and people were beginning to insinuate that this run-in must have been related to his pre-teen hustling. Marty's alternate goal was to control that narrative.

Mari sustained several injuries during the attack. He'd been stabbed twice in the chest, once in the stomach, and had sustained a two-inch gash on top of his right hand while trying to shield his stomach from another thrust of Max's blade. All told, the assault left Mari with fifty-nine stitches.

Prior to Mari's release, they received an update on Randy's condition from Cassidy, his mother. He had a slight concussion from hitting the floor but would be fine. Aside from that, he'd received seventeen stitches to close his three wounds. Thankfully, there would be no lingering physical issues. Mari and Randy spoke briefly before the moms hung up happy to hear that the other would be OK. They promised to get together later that week and ended the call with 'Love you, Man'.

That moment made Mari fondly remember the day they met. It was his third day in Pittsburgh. Mia had taken him to her gym. Randy had to rescue Mari who'd loaded the bar with too much weight and couldn't get it back onto the rack. He'd been trying to impress the ladies and failed miserably. Being the only other person their age at the gym, Mari and Randy decided to pair up. By the end of their workout, the two were horsing around and cracking jokes like old friends. It had been that way ever since. The pair had shared a lifetime of great memories since that chance encounter and had unfortunately added another unforgettable one.

THE FAMILY LEFT Pittsburgh General with Mari the following evening in silence with feelings ranging from shock and disbelief, to anger and confusion, to gratitude and vengeance. While there were no audible conversations, the silent discussions blared palpably throughout the vehicle. The thought that Mari could have been killed by that raving lunatic and that this all could have been avoided should Elaine and Ramon have come clean, was eating Darren up.

Every red light was met with interlocked fingers behind his head and deep, labored breathing. Mari finally broke the deafening silence and the slowed the simmering rage which could have easily permanently altered the loving family's dynamics. His statement was simple and so true to character. "I don't know about y'all, but a Brotha is in starvation mode. I need a Big

Mac, Mac DLT, a Quarter Pounder with some cheese, a filet-o-fish, a hamburger ..."

The atmosphere instantly lightened. That simple, goofy song was enough to reassure everyone that Mari was really going to be ok. The MRI showed that the inch-long box cutter hadn't perforated his stomach or any major organs. The chest wounds were near his heart, but thanks to benching over 350lbs three days a week, there was no damage beyond his pectorals. The surgeon did warn that the damage to his right hand had the potential of sidelining his football career. Mia and Darren thanked him for his help then they prayed that message away insisting that he'd start Physical Therapy to ensure he rebuilds properly, and that God would handle the rest.

With no McD's in sight, the family decided to pull into the next-best suitable option they could find close to Lothrop St. As the blonde, agile Sonic Girl skated her way to the black Escalade, both driver-side windows lowered in hungry anticipation with all occupants silently praying their meals wouldn't hit the ground before she handed them off. In no time, sounds of appreciation, mmms, and more mmms filled the air. The family was fully immersed, slurping, smacking, and licking fingers ⬜ too preoccupied to notice the black Cadillac that had pulled in two parking spots to their left.

.

CHAPTER 22:
In a Word – ACE

"EXCUSE ME, BRO," came a menacing voice through simultaneous taps on the driver's door window.

Darren lowered the window slightly.

"You got a light?" asked the voice's owner.

"No, we don't smoke," replied Darren cautiously noting the alcohol and tone in the question.

"You don't smoke? Ok. Is there anyone else in there who smokes and could help a brotha out?" retorted the man whose eyes began searching the Escalade. "Maybe that punk ass thief, J-Dog. My bad. I forgot. You go by Ja-Mar-EE Copeland nowadays." He laughed, then menacingly added, "I'm just saying, after coppin $45G's, *he should* have enough for a light."

At that moment, they noticed two additional shadows moving in the Cadillac and a man appeared on the passenger side. It was immediately known where this was going.

"That dealer?" whispered Elaine. "What was his name?" She wracked her brain trying to think of his name.

"Rosco," muttered Jamari. His pained voice reflecting anger, shame, and disbelief.

"You know it, playa," added another man speaking purposely to the back passengers. "And ya boy wants his funds back with interest. Seeing how it's been what? Five years since you've been holding that cash, I'm thinking we can settle this with...shit, let's say $60,000 and call it a day. Then you can go on about your football career and all."

"We don't have that money," said Mia. "It was given to the police years ago."

"Well, I guess you got a problem that needs figuring out — like real quick," said the first guy after taking a long drag from his freshly lit cigarette, and intentionally blowing the smoke into Darren's still cracked window. "You got 'til Friday. You two are big shot lawyers, right? In Essence Magazine and all. I'm sure you can find it."

"Are you sure you want to go there?" asked Darren. "You want to pick up charges for extortion of an officer, no two officers of the court. Those are Federal, baby boy. These little charges you might pick up peddling for what's his name, Rosco? These ain't nothing. With Federal charges, you can kiss your happy asses and your street-cred goodbye.

"And since you know us so well, you already know that Washington, Worthy, and Meyers makes sure that those who catch federal indictments are treated *really, really nice*. You won't be put in with the general population. Shit, we'll even make sure you get special accommodations. In fact, when we're done with your sorry asses, every dealer east of the Mississippi, including Rosco, will know how well you were treated while you were in lock-up."

Feeling an inexplicable courage, Darren unfastened his seatbelt and opened the door, much to everyone's horror and a plethora of objections. Once, outside of the vehicle, he found that he was taller than all but one of the men and his physique made them appear even smaller. Looking at each of the men, he continued, "Now, gentlemen, how do you think that'll play out for you on these streets?"

"You full of shit. Don't nobody believe that," said the first man taking a step towards Darren.

"You think so? Try me," spat Darren, eliminating what little space remained between them. "Oh, and I'll be sure to let the judge know how appreciative we were with your cooperation and the info that ALL OF YOU provided," he added making eye contact with each man. "So, here's what's going to happen. Y'all are gonna get back into that caddie and roll out. And I'd better not see either of you near this family again. Tell your boy whatever you need or even better, tell him to come holla at me personally. Oh, my bad. He's still locked up. What's he got, twenty-five more years?" Darren feigned a sinister chuckle and continued nodding towards the vehicle shielding his utterly petrified family.

"My father-in-law in there is an award-winning international photographer. Trust me, he's got each of your sorry ass mugshots and has uploaded them to his shared network. As soon as his peers log in tomorrow, they'll be there, unless you feel like walking away right now. I know at least one of you is on probation." Darren then looks back at the apparent leader of the quad. "Now, how do you want to play this, playa?"

That last statement scared Darren because he'd just repeated verbatim what his dad had said many times before to his disenfranchised partners and had felt the evil coolness that accompanied the statement. It was well-known that if Marshon Wilford asked that question, the respondent had better answer correctly as any other answer meant someone was going to die.

"Don't nobody care about that bullshit you're spitting."

In an instant, Darren was brought back to the current situation, but his father's ferocity stayed.

"But I tell you what. We're cool for now." Yelling menacingly into the vehicle, "Mari, I hope you feel better soon." Then turning back to Darren, with a deadly glare adds, "Shouldn't be too bad. Rosco told Max to just take a box cutter to him."

"I'mma ask you again," Darren spit through clenched teeth inserting himself between the man and the passengers still horrified behind the glass. "How you want to play this . . . Playa?"

The four men smiled and walked back to their vehicle. Darren maintained eye contact. Waving at the men, he echoed his warning regarding their preferential treatment behind bars. He winked at the group as the caddie and its chrome 22's sped off. Only after the taillights disappeared though the fifth light of The Avenue of the Ailles, did Darren allow himself to exhale and when he did, the gravity of the confrontation hit him head on. A million emotions competed for dominance as he collapsed into the back bumper.

Incredulously, he thought of his father, and had to credit his unwavering courage and ferocity even when cornered with saving him and his family this evening. Darren had watched his dad's ruthlessness in negotiations and stealth in spinning unparalleled bullshit when his back was against the wall. He'd even seen his father convince some Mexicans that they were responsible for a $500,000 shipment being seized by the police after it was already in his crew's possession.

As much as he hated to admit it, the years of watching his father's "art of persuasion" and negotiation tactics had been beneficial to him in life and in the courtroom. In fact, he drew on that knowledge and reveled in it. Darren easily owned a doctorate in precision and cunningness. He'd even earned the nickname, "Air Tight" amongst prosecutors as everyone knew cases had to be bullet-proof if he was the defense attorney. Darren was too smart. Too sharp. Too quick. And now, here he was using the only lesson he'd learned from his father to defend his family. Unfortunately, his father also possessed a kill-or-be-killed philosophy. A philosophy that after this incident, Darren fully understood.

"Darren? Sweetheart, answer me," exclaimed Mia after several failed attempts at trying to get his attention. Her normally bright, happy eyes now a cocktail of terror, anxiety, and relief. He couldn't speak over the tightening in his chest. He simply held his wife of two years tightly, resting his head on and kissing her growing belly as if assuring his son or daughter that everything was going to be ok.

Instantly, Darren rose from the bumper, hustled Mia to the passenger side, and quickly closed the door behind her. He leapt across the front of the black SUV and tore out of the parking lot.

CHAPTER 23:
In a Word – RECKONING

*E*VERYONE FILED OUT of the vehicle in utter silence and ascended the two flights of stairs to the Wilford residence avoiding the pools of Randy's blood which still stained their steps. The police had long since gone, having collected their required evidence. All that remained was the cleanup. Once safely inside the condo, Elaine busied herself with getting Mari comfortable and dismissing his apologies for having his preteen troubles resurface.

The family assured him that his past was the past and that everything he's done since then defined him. Ramon called Kerry to provide an update and check on the kids. They both thanked her again for helping out last-minute. Once the painkillers kicked in, Elaine and Ramon settled into the living room while Mia and Darren changed out of their blood-stained clothes.

—————～————

"FOUND IT!" EXCLAIMED Darren emerging from his office after having spent the last ten minutes feverishly searching drawer by drawer and ultimately recovering the packet from his office closet. In his hand was a large manila folder containing several envelopes. His eyes said it all. Mia knew that he'd heard what she'd heard during that exchange with the thugs. She recalled what he'd recalled. That unasked and sometimes nagging question had again been called to the surface. The time of reckoning had come . . .

"Elaine. We need to talk," asserted Darren with the tone of the attorney who knows his defendant is lying and has something to hide, but there was another level in his tone – a more ominous, no-nonsense tone. Elaine nodded her head without looking at him or Mia who had joined her husband's side. Darren knew both sides of this situation well. He'd been that defendant holding out for dear life, praying that things would go well without the full truth surfacing. Elaine left Ramon's side only long enough to pour a glass of wine and return to her spot on the comfy grey sectional.

"Mom, you told everyone that Mari had $25,000 in that flour container all those years ago. That man said that Mari had $45,000. Max is calling me his daughter."

Ramon's lack of reaction to those statements told the Wilfords that Elaine wasn't alone in this secret.

"What is going on, Elaine? Ramon? One of you needs to say something. Mari and Randy could have been killed. That fool has the nerve to be calling my child his grandbaby. The stress is putting Mia and our baby at risk and on top of that, four idiots rolled up on us in the middle of the night. Shit, they were probably at the hospital and followed us to . . ." Darren's voice trailed off as that realization washed over him. Mia's heart sank with dread as she knew that the possibility they'd been followed was very real. Feeling that familiar twinge in her lower belly, Mia winced and sat in the rocking recliner.

Elaine rushed to tend to Mia.

"NO!" screamed Mia. "Stay there and answer the question. Please, Mom. Dad? Somebody say something."

"There was $25,000 in the flour tin. That was true." Sighed Elaine. "You remember that a few months after you took Mari, I agreed to let Jordyn and Bria have their own rooms. I got Bria that white captain's bed, so Mari's old bed had to go. When I pulled up the mattress, I found another $20,000. I wanted to turn it in to the police, because I knew it was dirty, but Ramon and I still weren't back together and the extra money allowed me to cut back my hours at work. I put it in the safe in our garage and pulled a hundred here and there as needed. Rosco or whatever his name is, was in prison. I never thought that anyone was coming back for the money since he was head hauncho. It wasn't like he was going to tell the police where his money was."

"And Max calling me his daugh-?"

"I'll get it," said Darren in response to the ringing telephone.

"Hey Mike . . . What? When? . . . Oh no."

CHAPTER 24:
In a Word – RESET

BLUE SKY, DARKNESS. Men in uniform, darkness. A solitary light on the ceiling, darkness. Double doors, darkness. A cool breeze, darkness. Blurs of light green, darkness . . .

When she finally regained consciousness, Mia found herself in a small hospital room hooked up to multiple monitors with an IV uncomfortably taped down on her hand.

"Ashes to ashes. Dust to dust . . ." were the last words she'd heard before waking up in recovery. The last nine days had been a blur. First, the realization that there was something to Maxwell's rantings, her mom's admission to having kept $20,000 in drug money, followed by the sudden death of Geoff Meyers, the third partner of her beloved Washington, Worthy, and Meyers law firm. It was Geoff who'd discovered Mia pouring through the notes during the Joey Gaithen trial at midnight in only her second month at the firm. He'd listened intently to her thoughts and what she'd perceived as a slight variation in the prosecution's key witness – the first responding officer's – testimony.

Her hunch had borne fruit. It turned out that their client had been the unwitting scapegoat in a political cover-up that ultimately took down aldermen, police officials, state representatives, and even the governor's chief of staff. Joey Gaithen, their twenty-three-year-old defendant had been a political science Grad student facing twenty-five to forty years. Because of Mia's research and subsequent discoveries, Geoff had been able to get the Honorable Judge Cobble to grant a continuance. After re-interviewing witnesses and gaining additional testimonies, Geoff moved to drop the case against Joey.

The State agreed to dismiss the federal charges but did charge him with Criminal Negligence as Joey had admitted to setting up meetings and delivering what turned out to be bribery and extortion documents. Judge Cobble did find him guilty of that misdemeanor offence and sentenced Joey to one-year with credit for time served. Ultimately, Judge Cobble determined Joey was merely an eager college student who had landed his dream job and did whatever was asked.

It was this case and Geoff's constant praise of her research that truly opened the door for her at Washington, Worthy, and Meyers law firm.

"BABE. OH, THANK God," cried Darren as her eyes squinted though the ever-increasing brightness. His five o'clock shadow poorly hid his clenched jaw.

The agony in his expression let Mia know that the situation was serious. Fear gripped her body. She searched Darren's eyes for answers. "What happened?" Panic began setting in. "How did I get here? The baby?" she asked horrified, reaching for her belly and praying that she would still find that familiar fullness. Tears rolled down her cheek when she felt her still round belly and little Wilford responding to her firm pressing.

"Mia, you collapsed at the gravesite. You've been in and out for almost an hour. The baby is fine. They did an ultrasound and this is the monitor for the baby. As you can hear, the heartbeat is strong. The Dr. said the vitals are normal."

"If the baby is fine, what happened?" Her confusion was back. "Is there something wrong with me?"

"No, Babe. Your oxygen levels were low and your iron, B12, and B6 are low. They think it was stress and a combination of low vitamin levels that caused you to faint. They're going to keep you overnight for monitoring. Just know you'll be having liver for breakfast and there'll be extra doses of beets and spinach on your daily menu from here on out. We need to get that A Positive blood bursting with nutrients," Darren joked with a relieved chuckle, now that his wife and child were in the clear.

Pulling up a chair, Darren searched his wife's eyes while peering into her soul and pleading intently, "No more talk about Max. We're not talking to Elaine and Ramon about any of this crap until after the baby is here. The only thing that's important is our family. Your health. Our baby's health. You've got too much on your mind. We've got eight more weeks until we meet him or her. Nothing is worth risking your health. Do you understand?"

Mia's eyes were full of remorse. She had been obsessed with finding the truth. She knew her appetite had completely vanished and she hadn't been resting properly. Her every waking moment was consumed. Geoff's death simply caused her mind and body to short circuit. "I do. I'm so sorry, Darren," she said sorrowfully reaching for her husband.

"It's ok, baby. I got you. Let me handle this," he whispered. "You just rest."

Recognizing that he could have lost his wife and unborn child, he held her tightly and took a solid breath for the first time in what seemed like an eternity. The burning embers of anger and vengeance that he'd felt that night at Sonic began creeping back into his being. Truth be told, the feelings never fully went away following that encounter. He'd recently found himself haunted by those way-too-familiar dark, dangerous emotions. That hatred he'd known all-too intimately.

It came during his stint in Klattville, when he learned that his dad was pinning the two murders on him. It grew following his testimony in court when his dad spat that he'd never amount to anything. Darren had called upon that hatred as fuel on the football field, that passion in the classroom, and that burning energy throughout his decorated collegiate career. Since his pre-teen years, the anger and hatred had gone from an eternal blazing furnace, to pesky smoldering embers, to virtually non-existent flickers. This was largely due to Mable and Gary's enduring, unconditional love and nurturing.

Now, the emotions threatened to overtake him again. As he held his beautiful, equally tormented wife, Darren resolved that Hell was about to freeze over. He just had to wait out the birth of their son.

"Son." He beamed. The on-call OBGYN had unwittingly uttered "he's going to be fine" after pulling the concerned father-to-be into the hallway to discuss Mia and the baby's health.

CHAPTER 25:
In a Word – ARRIVAL

"I

T'S TOO EARLY, Mom. I don't understand, why did my water break?"

"I guess the little one is getting bored in there," Elaine soothed. "You're thirty-six weeks. It's early, but not terrible."

While en route to the hospital, Elaine listened as Mia prayed earnestly. Until a few years ago, God was a mystery to Elaine. No one in her family had a relationship with Him while she was growing up, and as an adult, she'd gotten busy raising children. Elaine had never thought to seek Him. She did have the kids say grace before eating and prayers before bed because she was taught to do so, but that was pretty much it.

Now, Elaine found herself comfortably asking God for yet another act of mercy as she raced through the city.

Once checked in, Elaine again reassured Mia that the baby would be fine. She was there to calm Darren who was stuck on the turnpike due to a twelve-car pile-up.

Elaine handled the situation like a pro, after all, she'd been there five times herself. She'd been air traffic control that day – seamlessly coordinating calls, relaying information, timing contractions, and rubbing Mia's throbbing back. Darren arrived in Mia's fifth hour of labor and an hour into her pushing.

"Mia, it's really important that you push hard," urged Cindy, the Labor and Delivery nurse. "I know you're tired, but you have to push. On the next contraction, push HARD!"

"Mia, push, baby. You can do it," encouraged Darren who had assumed midwife duties and was now at her side holding one of her shivering legs.

She pushed with all that she had for another fifteen minutes before her heart rate began dropping.

"Mia. Stop pushing." her friendly, stocky doctor stated firmly. Having been through hundreds of deliveries with Dr. Orstern, the nurse immediately grabbed the oxygen, looping the mask behind each ear and pressing the call button on the wall near the hospital bed. She knew his next statement before he said it. "Call the OR, Cindy. Let them know we're on our way up for an emergency C-Section." The former collegiate gymnast turned OGBYN quickly explained the next steps to the petrified family as they prepped Mia to leave the room. Just then, the baby's heart rate began dropping.

"We have to go NOW!"

Mia was hustled out of the comfy, private delivery room and into the long tan corridor where she, Cindy, and the orderlies disappeared behind the cold, metal elevator doors.

Through it all, Elaine had been the pillar. While completely terrified, she didn't show it. She was the strength that Darren and Mia needed. She comforted Ramon who'd been out of town shooting the Regional Breast Cancer Walk-A-Thon.

"It figures," Ramon uttered with equal doses of aggravation and anguish.

Elaine assured Ramon that Mia would be fine. She also reminded him how he'd ended up as the third patient during Mia's own high-drama delivery. They'd said a prayer together while Mia was shuttled down to the Operating Room.

Fast forward to today, this experience had drawn the women closer. Mia respected and adored Elaine so much more than ever before. While there were nagging questions that she needed answering, she now fully understood how a mother would do anything to protect her child — even if it meant withholding truths.

"I DON'T UNDERSTAND why you're calling me about this, Chelly. And this matters to me because? I don't give a damn. They can dip him in acid and peel his skin off with a Brill-O Pad for all I care. . . . Consider what? Why the hell would I do that?" With that, the attention of the entire office had been turned towards the southwest corner of the building where Marty's office was.

In his twenty-two years at the firm, Marty had never uttered so much as a "gosh, darn it" and had rarely raised his voice. Now, he had cursed twice within two minutes of equally uncharacteristically high-decibel dialog. While the office was thoroughly perplexed and concerned about the outbursts coming from the normally Zen-like fourth floor office, they understood that whomever he was speaking with was better off swimming upstream in Class 5 rapids. Whatever was being asked was unacceptable and he was getting more annoyed with each passing second.

"Which part are you not understanding, Chelly? I really do not care," he growled. . . "Is that right? Well, if he does, *then* you call me. I'll make sure I'm there to light him on fire before he strolls through the gates. I mean it, Sis. You know I love you, but don't call me with nonsense about Max ever again. . . Ok, love you too."

As the phone landed on the receiver, the office staff realized that they and time had been standing still since Marty's initial outburst. Instantly, everyone resumed sending the emails, discussing their cases, and reviewing the manuals that had been neglected for the last several minutes. Moments later, another phone call. "Martin Worthy."

"Hi, Marty, it's Darren. It's a boy!"

———————◦—————

"OH, DARREN, HE'S beautiful," sobbed Mable. Gary looked over his wife's shoulder as she cradled their beautiful grandson. Gary wiped his own tears while marveling at the 5-pound 3-ounce bundle of joy.

"Daniel Gary Wilford. I love his name, son." Gary choked back his own tears. "I'm so proud of you and happy for you both." With that, he hugged Darren for the eightieth time and bent to kiss Mia who was reclining in the lounger still smarting from her emergency cesarean only two weeks earlier.

Moments later, little Danny's cry told the experienced Mable and Elaine that he was hungry. The men headed into the kitchen as the two first-time grandmas helped Mia adjust so that she could nurse her baby boy more comfortably. This would be Mable's last day with Daniel before she and Gary headed off to a missionary trip to Haiti and she took advantage of every moment. She would only put Danny down long enough to hit the restroom or to let Mia nurse. Elaine knew that due to Mable and Gary's distance and constant travels, she'd have much more time with her grandson, so she indulged her silver-haired counterpart allowing her to love on the tiny infant as much as possible.

With the baby fed, burped, and safely back in Mable's arms, Elaine helped Mia re-bandage her incision. She was so thankful for her mom's help. She honestly didn't know how she would have made it without her.

"YEAH, WE'RE HERE. Yeah. Weeboy Manor. Come on by whenever. Looking forward to seeing you too." Darren smiled as he hung up his phone still amazed at all of the love they've been receiving lately from various members of the criminal justice community. It was the first Saturday in July and life couldn't have gotten any better. Mia was suffering from cabin fever and thought it would be great to visit and relax at Marty's lodge. After all, with all of the visitors crowding into their condo, their normally spacious abode had begun to feel claustrophobic.

Darren popped the top off of three beers and the

men serendipitously clanged their bottles. "You're a dad," exclaimed Gary. "I know you're going to be amazing. You're amazing at everything you do and I can't wait to see you tackle this role."

"Yeah, puffy-eyed, sleep-deprived, delirious, and runnin' on E 24/7," laughed Ramon. "I tell you what, enjoy every moment because he'll be asking for those keys in no t-. . ." Ramon's statement was cut off by a sudden, urgent pounding at the huge solid wooden front doors followed by, "Let me in! I want to see my grandson!"

CHAPTER 26:
In a Word – MELEE

MASS CHAOS ENSUED as Gary, Ramon, and the 101 pound, 5'1" Mable tried futilely to stop the equally incensed Elaine and Darren from breaking the 8' double doors down from the inside. Meanwhile, Mia scrambled as quickly as possible into the rustic kitchen with baby Daniel; the pain in her abdomen searing from her sudden motions. Every fiber in her body wanted to confront Max, but not in her current state. She wanted to be strong enough to hit him with at least three of her five most potent Krav Maga moves.

Gary threw himself between Darren and the door imploring him not to turn the knob. Instead, he reminded his beloved son of his career, loving wife, and new baby who needed him there, not in prison or dead. Darren acknowledged Gary's advice, and with eyes intently blazing, asked him to move. "This needs to end – now!"

On the other side of the door was the impatient and

unapologetically ignorant Max who had been bonded out on his $2,000,000 bail two days prior. With him were two of the four goons from their frightening late-night encounter months earlier.

Once outside, arguing ensued. Punches were thrown. Guns were drawn and shots pierced the sunbaked afternoon air. Max flew off the balcony from the force of Elaine's .22, which she'd drawn whilst all attention was focused on keeping Darren inside the safety of the two-story log cabin. Max was hit in the chest. Darren dropped to his knees as a bullet pierced his side. Another shot rang out from the driveway. It was Eddie Carpenter, AKA Judge Carpenter. It was him who'd called Darren minutes ago asking if they were up for company.

The judge had heard that Max made bail and wanted to deliver the news in person. For a still undetermined reason, a couple of Senators in New York and Chicago had a particular interest in seeing Max released and pulled a few strings while Marty and Mike were on safari in Zimbabwe with their families. The fact that Darren and Mia were unaware clearly meant that the word had not yet reached the vacationing partners.

Instead of exiting his red Ford F250 with the flowers and baby gift intended to celebrate the joyous occasion, the Judge stepped out with his trusty Glock freshly extracted from his lower glove compartment.

Eddie Carpenter was an expert marksman, having been a decorated sniper while serving as a Marine in his youth. The Judge had intentionally missed the two recently released convicts when firing due to his political stature but made it crystal-clear in his pervasive southern twang that if he had to fire again, the next shots would be escorting them both into their next lives.

With full understanding that they were not winning today's fight, both put their hands up and lay on the ground. The earth seemed to exhale as relief began washing over the cabin's visitors. Adding to the release were the faintest sounds of sirens racing in their direction. Unlike their last recollection of the sirens, these were accompanied by the rhythmic thunder of choppers in the distance. Apparently, a panicked 9-1-1 call with reports of shots fired from one of the most exclusive gated waterfront properties on the east coast, which happened to be owned by one third of the WW&M law firm, was worthy of media attention.

The menacing trio had gotten onto the Weeboy property via an old cave near the water's edge that the Worthy brothers discovered as children. Legend had it that this cave had been the path to freedom in the North for hundreds of slaves. Unfortunately, it was the same cave that Weeboy's parents had drowned in after pushing him through. Their bodies had been found shortly after Andrew spotted Weeboy. Both had been buried at the edge of the property near the massive Weeping Willow.

The monstrous arbor was visible in the distance as Judge Carpenter and Elaine held guns on the two thugs while Gary and Mable tended to Darren. Maxwell was ashen from an almost lethal combination of shock and blood loss from the hole in his upper torso. He'd begun losing his battle with death when Gary got to him and applied pressure slowing the bleeding. A defiant instigator 'til the end, Max's last words before surrendering to darkness were aimed squarely at Elaine, "You know that's my grandchild."

Gary and Judge Carpenter glanced over at Elaine who was incredulous. She couldn't believe his brazenness. After all these years. Her hands were now shaking so much from anger that the judge commanded her to give him her gun. The normally comforting southern twang was replaced by a decidedly no-nonsense military tone. His main concern of course, was that she'd accidentally shoot someone with her incessant shaking.

"Yeah, take the gun before I accidentally empty it in him," scoffed Elaine. She handed her piece to the judge and ran into the house to check on Mia and baby Daniel.

"Amazing grace, how sweet the sound that saved a wretch like me. . ." Mia whispered the lullaby to her baby boy. By this time, she was lying on the white hickory kitchen floor too weak to stand. That searing pain she'd felt when jumping out of the rocker with the baby and hurrying into the kitchen was her C-section reopening. While only a few minutes had passed since Max's knock and subsequent outburst, she'd lost enough blood to be in imminent danger. The baby lay peacefully at his mother's side, completely oblivious to the fact that his mom and dad were both in serious trouble.

"Lord, I trust You. I thank You for this beautiful boy. I thank You for my loving husband and I thank You for keeping us. I don't want to leave them now, but if it's

Your will, I am ready. I know that You have favored and covered, Darren and Daniel and I thank You for calling them yours," she prayed weakly.

"Mia!" Elaine screamed upon finding her in an ever-increasing pool of blood and yelled for Mable. The former Emergency Room nurse hurried into the kitchen. Though retired for five years, the knowledge, expertise, and muscle memory immediately kicked in. She instantly began assessing and talking to Mia, doing her best to keep her alert and calm until the EMTs arrived.

Ambulances rushed Darren, and Max to the hospital. Police questioned Judge Carpenter and Elaine about their weapons and the shots fired. Other officers interrogated Gary and Ramon as crime scene tape began stretching across the sprawling landscaping. Helicopters hovered above while local media trucks lined the lengthy driveway with antennas stretched into the sky.

CHAPTER 27:
In a Word – ENDURE

"*H*AWKEYE 67 INBOUND. ETA six minutes. We are transporting a thirty-three-year-old African American female. She is two-weeks post-partum. Patient's cesarean incision is severely ruptured and she has substantial bleeding."

As fate would have it, Mable had retired from UPMC's Emergency Department. While on the line with a 9-1-1 dispatcher, Mable provided her credentials and implored the dispatch to send 'a bird'. She explained that she'd seen enough critical cases in her time to know that Mia needed an air flight.

The pilot continued providing updates to the hospital's dispatch. "Patient is A+ and has received two liters of blood —"

"Her pulse is gone," yelled the flight nurse.

"Paddles. Clear. . . Nothing. Increase to 300. Clear . .

. Still nothing," reported the in-flight physician. "Increase to 500."

"Come on Amia. You've got a beautiful baby boy who needs you," urged the flight nurse as she adjusted the voltage.

"Clear. . . Ok, we have a pulse. Great job, Amia. Hang in there," said the relieved physician as he patted her shoulder."

"We have a pulse," reiterated the pilot to dispatch. "ETA is four minutes."

"A team of orderlies met the orange helicopter on the hospital's roof bracing themselves against the blade-driven winds to rush the critically ill Mia into surgery.

Minutes later, a screeching ambulance speeds into UPMC's ER.

"Let's go people. Make a hole," yelled the EMTs as they rushed Darren past the media who'd been alerted that all three of the victims of the Weeboy Manor shooting were being rushed to UPMC. They'd staked the most opportune location to capture the ambulances' arrival and were waiting with bulbs flashing.

The three techs began spouting vitals to the awaiting attendees in the bright, now extremely chaotic emergency room.

"Gunshot victim. We've been able to slow the bleeding, but he is critical. BP is now 69 over 35. IV fluids have been started. We are unable to locate an exit wound."

Darren faded in and out of consciousness. The only coherent words that the staff could discern were 'My Wife' and 'My son'. Each time, the attendees would assure the disoriented husband and father that his family would be fine. Unfortunately, he had lost too much blood to aid in his own care and couldn't answer any of their questions. Gary who'd ridden in the ambulance, did his best to fill in the gaps.

"His blood type is B negative. His name is Darren Wilford. He's a Defense Attorney here in Pittsburgh," then he implored the staff, "Please take care of my son. He's the only one I have."

"The staff remained professional though their confusion was evident — after all, their patient was clearly a Black man and Gary clearly was not.

"We will Sir," the younger red-haired physician caringly replied as he escorted Gary just outside of the room.

"We are sending him up to surgery. There's not an exit wound and we need to find that bullet. We need to remove it if possible and try to fix whatever damage has been done. We're going to do everything we can." With that, the slim friendly man slipped back behind the curtain and began ordering next steps.

"Call the OR. Let them know we've got a gunshot wound to the abdomen with no exit. We don't have time for a CT. There are likely multiple internal injuries. He'll need exploratory surgery. Request seven units of O Positive." Though Gary advised that Darren was B negative, the ER staff knew enough to have O positive administered until they could verify the blood type for themselves.

Days later, Darren was wheeled into Amia's room for his first glance of his wife following that devastating afternoon. The trauma surgeon had to remove Darren's spleen which had been lacerated by the round. Thankfully, he was also able to extract the bullet which he'd found lodged in Darren's ribcage.

Jamari left Mia's side long enough to carefully hug Darren again. Darren studied his sleeping wife with tubes and wires everywhere.

"Does she know," asked Darren while stroking her hand and choking down his anguish."

"Not yet, answered Mari solemnly."

"Mr. Wilford, we need to get you back to your room now. I could lose my job if you're not back in that bed in ten minutes," added the orderly. That part wasn't true, but the orderly had dealt with patients with dual family admissions enough to know that leveraging his job was usually enough to get patients to return to their rooms.

"Two more minutes," he replied while kissing her unresponsive hand.

"Please, Mari. Don't let anyone say anything. I want to tell her."

CHAPTER 28:
In a Word – PAINS

"SO, HOW DOES it feel to be back at home after eight days?" asked Mari. He'd remained in the city after getting the news, missing the first two weeks of football camp to be at his family's side.

"I'm thankful, but it's strange," answered Darren still wincing from the surgery. "How's the hand? I noticed at the hospital that you're out of the hard brace. Looks like a soft removable one now."

"Yeah, the docs cleared me the day before everything went down at Weeboy. I'll be wearing this new brace for another month or so. It's much better and I now have full range of motion and some grip. I just have to get my strength back. Oh, and I did tell you that I get to keep my scholarship, even though I'm red-shirting this year, right?"

"What? That's a blessing, boy," Darren said reaching out to give him a hug.

"Owww!" Darren screamed, instantly remembering that his side and ribcage were still unappreciative of any sudden movements."

"You just held him. It's my turn to hold him. Daddddd!" yelled Bria angry that Jordyn was again holding their precious nephew.

"Knock it off, you two," replied Elaine who could officially breathe a sigh of relief now that she was not going to be charged with attempted murder for critically wounding Max. She'd applied for the concealed carry permit following the Keys to the City ceremony. Though assured by everyone that no charges would be filed, she refused to allow herself to believe it until this morning's decision.

While that was great news for the family, they still ached for Mia and Darren who were grappling with another devasting blow.

Only four days earlier, Darren gingerly climbed into Mia's bed and broke the news to her. He revealed that the surgeons did all they could to stop her bleeding, but after the fourth transfusion and still unsuccessfully repairing the tear, they abandoned their goal of saving her uterus and her life, instead focusing solely on saving her life.

They cried together as he told her that they'd removed her womb. They lay in silent heartbreak at the idea that they would never again experience the miracle of their baby's gymnastics routines while lying in bed at night. Darren would never kiss her full belly or give life lessons in utero ever again.

Mia wailed openly at the thought of Daniel never having a baby sister or brother; at least, not one that she would carry. Her heart ached knowing that she would never nurse another baby. Sadly, there would be no more baby showers, no 'Little Darren'. There would be no little girl for him to spoil as much as Ramon had spoiled her.

Mia recalled their friendly debate one evening while planning their next pregnancy. She had been seven months along with Daniel and was insistent that she be pregnant during the winter so that she could wear a cute maternity coat that she'd found on the clearance rack at Saks. Because she'd delivered Daniel in the summer, she never got to wear it. Darren half-smiling remembered his disbelief that a green and yellow checkered garment was dictating the terms of their next child's arrival.

Through the heartache of that day and in the hours since, they'd been each other's anchor. The Wilford's were hurt – physically, emotionally, and yes, even spiritually. They spent equal parts of the day in the other's room sometimes in painful silence. Other moments were spent ever more in love with each other as God allowed them to see their shared strength and vulnerability. He let them experience filling each other's voids and be each other's help. Mia and Darren realized that the 'worse' in 'for better or for worse', was bearable so long as they had each other.

Now they were home and adjusting to their new normal. Their families had been a tremendous help throughout the ordeal. All that was left now that they were healing was to learn the secret behind the recent life-altering events.

Ramon paid the pizza delivery lady and ignored the reporters shouting questions for comment. "When are they going to go away?" he mused.

"Maybe after they get some answers to their questions," chimed Jamari. The sharp edge and double meaning not missed by anyone. Darren wheeled his chair into their family room, which now serves as their master bedroom until they can each manage ascending and descending their condo's winding staircase.

"Yes, they deserve the truth."

Everyone's attention turned towards Kerry, Elaine's best friend. Walking over to Elaine and Ramon, she urged them to share the secret that had been paining them for over 30 years. As Elaine's best friend, she'd known from the start. Ramon's best friend, Arturo, who he'd met while imbedded with the Special Forces, had taken their secret to his grave. The fearless Ranger, Ramon's partner in crime, had been tragically killed years earlier during an ambush in Kosovo.

Though she'd been at Mia and Darren's home for the past few days, it was still hard to recognize Kerry. Since the kids had known her, she was the hazel-eyed quiet beauty with the envious waist-length curly mane. Her color was so beautiful that everyone tried (unsuccess-fully) to replicate the naturally reddish-brown tresses. Now Kerry's curls were cropped into the cutest jet-black pixie.

Having loved Elaine and Ramon forever, Kerry could feel their anguish. Guiding them each to sister chairs at the base of the bed, she assured them that it would be OK. Mia sat in her bed propped gingerly with pillows. Her facial expression too hard to interpret due to the rollercoaster of emotions that had defined her life lately. Darren wheeled over to Mia's side. Mari announced that he would put on a movie for the kids.

The doorbell rang as he popped the last bag of popcorn and began going over the rules with his younger siblings. To his surprise, it was Marty and his wife, Victoria. Interestingly, of the adults, only Mia and Darren were surprised to see them. It seemed as though Ramon, Elaine, and Kerry were expecting the pair as they anxiously greeted and motioned them to the reupholstered oversized ottoman.

Also curious were Marty and Victoria's demeanor. They knew something too. Even in their codeine-induced states, this was easily perceived by Mia and Darren who were alternately searching everyone's faces for clues. Mari returned announcing that the kids were squared away.

Five Mississippi, Six Mississippi, Seven Mississippi, Eight Mississippi . . . No one wanted to speak first.

"Someone please start talking," implored Darren.

Elaine finally managed to find her voice, "I'll start."

"Just a yes or a no, please. Is Maxwell Worthy my father?"

"Probably. And it's my fault," added Marty.

CHAPTER 29:
In a Word – MERCY

"*T*HANK YOU. ENJOY your flight." Smiled the gate attendant whose adoring gaze lingered on Darren long enough to make the entire terminal blush.

"I think he likes you," joked Mia.

"Go 'head with that girl," retorted Darren. "He playin' way too much. The pilot needs to get us in the air ASAP. That brotha got me watching my back."

They both shared a belly laugh as they sauntered down the grey jet way towards their next adventure. It had been just over four years since the dramatic confessions which led to Amia having to revisit everything she'd known about her family up to that moment.

She and Darren were just returning from celebrating Jamari's graduation. Although no one questioned his abilities, it was still hard to believe that this kid, Jamari Copeland and all that he'd overcome, was now the proud owner of a BS in Sociology from Penn State. On top of that, he'd proposed to his college sweetheart, Michelle, during his fun-filled, nostalgic graduation party. The partners at Washington, Worthy & now Wilford had all thrown the bash for Mari in the annex of their newest location, opened on the northside of the city.

Randy who'd sustained a career-ending back injury at the beginning of his Junior year at Ohio State was there along with his very heavily pregnant fiancée. They'd risked the three-hour journey to be at Mari's graduation and after-party. In addition, friends and family came from all corners.

Little Danny never left Mari's side during the entire event and figured out how to get some part of his rugged, adorable body into almost every photo.

He would stay behind following the party to spend two weeks split between Uncle Marty and Aunty V's and "Ma-Ma" and "Pop's" – Elaine and Ramon insisted he call them by those monikers as "Grand" anything had been strictly prohibited. Danny would be reaping the fruits of being an utterly adorable four-year-old while his mom and dad spent two weeks unwinding in picturesque Awahu. It would be their last vacation before expanding their young family.

The ink was dry. The papers were finalized. Their adoption agency had matched them with a twenty-eight-year-old who had found herself unexpectedly pregnant. According to the woman, the father was a "complete loser" and she had no interest in keeping the child or being a single mother. While the adoption would be closed meaning, Mia and Darren would not know the birth mom, she was able to see their profiles and quickly decided that her baby had been meant for Darren and Mia. They would be bringing home their precious baby, Christina, right after her birth at the end of the month.

These past few years were a blur. Mia had learned that Maxwell was indeed her father. Bits and pieces were revealed when the family converged on Mia and Darren's home after they'd been released from the hospital following the bloody shootout. Maxwell Worthy and his two henchmen having obviously violated the terms of their various paroles were returned to prison.

Darren had been offered partnership at the firm not long after that. He'd accepted, but with the stipulation that they open a largely pro-bono and reduced-fee branch to better serve the entire community. That new division also included partnerships with law enforcement who would tutor and mentor kids in an effort to bolster community relations. There was a strong focus on victim advocacy, victims' rights and education.

IN THE MONTHS and years between the 'Come to Jesus' meeting at their 2658 Windber Ave. condo and the decision to adopt came exponential growth and healing for one Amia J. Wilford. She routinely struggled with her infertility and the shame of it began threatening her sunshine.

"But how can he love me the same, Dr. P? I can't give him any more babies. We intentionally delayed having kids until marriage and now. . . Darren deserves to have more kids. He's an amazing dad. I feel like he might be staying with me out of pity." Mia would repeat this deep-seated fear in every biweekly therapy session which she'd sought to deal with the trauma of her sudden barrenness following her emergency hysterectomy.

The therapist, a very tall, built woman who had clearly dominated on the basketball court at some point in her youth, was just what she needed. She'd been recommended by the First Lady at Mia's church. That was one thing that she loved about her ministers. They preached healing and leaning on the Lord.

They also wanted their congregation to embrace health and engage with the medical community since many of their members were healthcare professionals with undeniable God-given talents. In fact, the First Lady was a licensed RN. One of her favorite sayings was, "God does the supernatural. You do the natural. God is the healer. You do what you need to do to facilitate your healing."

With that and Darren's encouragement, twice a week for about nine months, Mia would coil up in the corner of the deep, cozy seafoam green sofa and share her feelings of inadequacy, which Dr. Paxton met with adequate doses of scripture and reasoning.

"You know that's a lie from the pit of Hell," Dr. P would say, addressing each worry. "Bearing children does not make you more or less of a woman. That wonderful guy that you married loved you before he ever saw you carrying his child. He got to enjoy the highs and lows of your pregnancy with Daniel and if he never gets to do it again with you, he will still be happy – and deep down, Amia Wilford, you know it." Dr. P's voice, while tinged with rasp from years of therapizing, always oozed wisdom and sincerity.

Darren even jokingly informed Mia that Hell would freeze over, Earth would reverse rotation, and he would breakdance naked in front of Judge Haverhill before he would ever stop loving her. Still, Mia's feelings of defect were causing her to shy away from intimacy with her husband. She knew she wouldn't be giving him more children and as weird as it sounded, she hadn't wanted him to feel robbed by having sex with her. Mia desperately wanted to spare Darren the disappointment of depositing seeds that would never grow again. During that time of brokenness, intimacy always ended with Mia shedding tears of inadequacy.

Then, one morning, a breakthrough. Darren was preparing for practice as Mia finished feeding Daniel. The football that he'd tucked under his armpit fell onto the bed causing the little one to unlatch. Instead of continuing to nurse after finding the source of the noise, the ten-month old reached for the football.

"That's my boy," he beamed. "I knew when you were in mommy's tummy that you would pick up a football before you started walking."

Mia smiled lovingly at her baby and took a mental picture of her loving husband sharing his love of football with their son. And then it hit her —.

"Oh my God, Babe. God knew when I was born that Daniel would be the only child I would carry. He was not surprised when Max showed up, or when I ripped the incision, or when they removed my uterus. He was not surprised."

"No, He wasn't."

"I don't like that fact at all and I don't understand why God would allow this level of devastation to be written into our life story. Honestly, I still don't think it's fair. We have so many gifts to share. Babe, I can't see you with only one child."

"Mia," he replied while kissing Daniel's cheek. "I don't understand it either and it still hurts when I think about it, but I do know that if He allowed this to be part of our plan, He's got something amazing in store for us."

"Your latter will be greater than your past, right?"

"That's what Haggi 2:9 says," he smiled.

"Babe. . . . We are beyond blessed. I mean pressed down, shaken together, running over blessed. I hate that I won't ever be pregnant again and I hate that I won't get to wear that coat," she managed. The pained thought brought a tear to her eye.

"But you know what," she asked with resolution quickly wiping the tear away. "If the trade-off for God sparing every one of us that afternoon at Weeboy is me not carrying another child, I'm gonna take that deal — all day, every day!"

That revelation changed everything. The pair's collective hearts were again filled with joy and awe at the goodness of God. Though they'd never stopped going to church throughout the ordeal, their excitement had waned. Until that point, the pair had been surviving on fumes. It was their faith that kept them going — literally and figuratively.

Mia fully returned to her husband that morning. She embraced Darren's dedication and allowed herself to enjoy making love to him again. This time, though, she was able to fully release and immerse herself in the beauty that God had created it to be. Gone was the shame of infertility. There was no longer an ulterior motive when they came together. It was just her and Darren with limbs inextricably entwined physically professing their undying love for each other.

Soon after that breakthrough, Mia and Dr. Paxton's discussions turned to Maxwell Worthy, Mia's other source of angst. Originally, Mia feared broaching the topic but she was a child of God, no matter whose blood coursed through her veins. Mia would lean on this reminder regularly as there were some tough truths charging down the horizon.

CHAPTER 30:
In a Word – DEPOSITION

MARTY ENCOURAGED ELAINE to petition the State of California to ensure Max never got to see the light of day ever again. A few short years later, she, Ramon, Mia and Darren traveled with him to the Golden State. Normally, visiting California and its endless miles of sun-kissed beaches would garner excitement and anticipation. Unfortunately, this was not that kind of trip. They would spend a few difficult days within the confines of the State House. It would be here that the world would learn the full, sordid details of her conception.

"Do you swear to tell the truth, the whole truth, and nothing but the truth so help you God."

"I do." With those two simple words, Elaine began recalling her encounter with Max over thirty years ago. While on the stand, Elaine revealed that she'd caught Ramon kissing another woman while they were on Spring Break in California. Ramon contended that the coed had seduced him. He admitted that he'd initially returned the kiss but was cutting it off as Elaine turned the corner and witnessed their lips still locked.

She confessed that she decided to get even and had sought out anyone with which to get back at him. Elaine had met Max while storming out of the gymnasium in such a fury that she'd almost knocked him over. She flirted with him long enough for Ramon to overhear Max giving her his number. He apologized continuously and begged Elaine to forgive him, but she was having none of it.

"Later that evening, I met Max at an off-campus cookout, which was hosted by his younger brother, Martin, Elaine explained.

As the last partygoers left, Marty realized that they'd run out of alcohol and food. His friends had planned to crash on the couch, so the trio left the tiny three-bedroom home to pick up more eats.

"I wasn't nearly as mad at Ramon anymore," she revealed, "but I was still hurt by him and me being me, I was going to ensure that I got him back in some way.

"Not long after they left, I started flirting with Max. It's not something I would normally do, but I was bolstered by the wine coolers and flattered that a college guy was interested in me. I'm embarrassed to say that we had an intense make-out session in the kitchen.

"We slowly made it to one of the bedrooms when I came to my senses. In that moment, I apologized and admitted that I had no interest in having sex with Max. I told him that I was disappointed in Ramon, but still loved him," she said dabbing her eyes.

"And deep down," she confessed to the jury, "I knew I shouldn't have even been there. Ramon wouldn't have cheated on me and I knew that."

Then she continued, "Max acted as if he understood and politely left the room. I stood there for two minutes bouncing between scolding myself and being relieved that he understood. But it didn't sit right with me. My gut told me that he'd given up too soon, but I ignored it and eventually walked back into the kitchen where he was. As I rounded the corner, I found him turning to pour two cups of alcohol from a bottle that had been stashed in a cupboard above the fridge.

"If I'm being honest, it felt wrong. I didn't make sense that this bottle had been tucked away from all of the other alcohol. He handed me a white styrofoam cup and offered a toast to us being friends. I actually heard myself tell me not to drink it. Plus every cell in my body was screaming at me, but I chose to drown out the warnings. My instincts have always been spot on, but I was embarrassed by my actions. I raised the cup to my lips. The fumes almost burned my nostrils, but I didn't want to look like a bigger idiot in front of this college guy, so I took a sip.

"The whole time, Max was tapping the bottom of the cup encouraging me to chug it. I'd drank hard alcohol once before and knew I didn't like the taste. I took a few big sips, hoping that he'd be happy. Again, my instincts told me something was wrong when I noticed that he never actually took a sip from his white cup." Elaine's tears were now freefalling.

"I remember feeling loopy and lightheaded almost immediately. I didn't fully understand what why, but I knew I needed to get out of that house immediately. I just couldn't."

She couldn't because curves and bends had begun replacing the previously straight green lines that had been crisscrossing into large diamonds on the wallpaper.

"I wasn't an athlete, but my legs were athletic but couldn't hold me up any longer. I struggled to hold onto reality."

Because Elaine hadn't drank all of the beverage, she'd avoided the ultimate goal of the roofies and never lost consciousness. She told the jury that she still wasn't sure if that had been a blessing or a curse.

"It sounds crazy, but I can remember watching myself being dragged backwards into a different bedroom. I remember that it was dimly lit and he was barking at me repeatedly, calling me names. I heard him say that girls like me had to learn not to play games and..." she paused and locked eyes with Ramon whose heart was breaking for his wife – "swore that I would never, ever do it again."

Elaine revealed in court that though together for two years, she and Ramon had never had sex – though not for religious reasons. Elaine had grown up as the youngest of eight children. They never had enough to eat or good shoes to wear because there were so many mouths to feed. She knew she wanted a big family, but did not want that for her children. Ramon was the opposite. His family had plenty of money, but his parents argued all the time in front of he and his brothers.

They also had kids before they wanted. Ramon made up his mind that he would not have any children until he was sure that he'd found the right one and while he was pretty sure Elaine was right for him, the only way to ensure she didn't get pregnant before he was completely certain was not to have sex with her. The couple vowed not to engage in it until they were married and were ready for kids. Sure, they'd made out and had even done some heavy petting throughout their relationship, but it never went any further.

"It felt like I was drunk. Like I wasn't screaming and fighting under Max's weight, but I was trying. I kept trying to hang onto the clothes that he was stealing from my body, but my arms weren't responding. My hands couldn't grip. My legs felt like logs. All I could think of was Ramon and how I would have given anything to be back at the gym with him."

Elaine revealed that she'd apologized repeatedly for leading him on and begged Max to let her leave the home. Her pleas seemed to anger and excite him as he'd intensified his assault. Dread and panic ensued as the unmistakable sound of his zipper ripped through her ears. Her desperate, drugged screams gave way to heartbreaking groans as he forced himself roughly inside. She sobbed intensely as she recalled his hot, alcohol laden breath on her neck as he pounded away her virginity. Decades later, she still mourned at her naivete and its destruction of her innocence.

"Eventually, I gave up and just hoped for a quick end to the onslaught. I focused on the leafy shadows of swaying the oak tree in their front yard as he finished. I remember being grateful that it was over. I couldn't really move, but it didn't panic me as much because I figured he would just leave after getting what he wanted."

By this time, Elaine's emotion was almost as raw as it had been decades earlier. The judge called for a brief recess to give every person in the courtroom a chance to regain their composure which had all but dissolved. Several jurors wept silently for the innocent nineteen-year-old who'd been so vividly resurrected during Elaine's time on the stand.

Ramon and Mia held hands as Elaine relived that night of terror. He'd have given anything to have torn up those round-trip tickets to California but he couldn't – and wouldn't because their precious daughter came from that night.

Grateful for a break in the proceedings, Mia exited the courtroom in search of solace. She tucked into a corner ledge of the courthouse's golden bronze pergola and let the sun's rays soothe her soul. She'd heard the story several times prior to today as she personally prepped Elaine for her testimony. As impossible as it was to hear the details, there was no way Mia was letting anyone else prepare her mother to testify against Maxwell.

In the beginning, Elaine desperately resisted Mia's pressure for specifics as she wanted nothing more than to spare her daughter the hurt that they would surely cause. She was right. Learning the minutiae was downright painful. They struggled – Elaine with speaking her truth and Mia with hearing it. Still, Mia insisted that they keep at it. By the fifteenth session, the details no longer stung. Instead, everything was matter of fact. Interestingly, the sessions had an unexpected side effect for both women – catharsis. Mia closed her eyes exhaling deeply as the rays continued to warm her skin.

"Babe, you ok?" asked a concerned Darren who'd finally found her after minutes of searching the building.

Mia smiled lovingly at her handsome soul mate. Even now, she still couldn't believe that God had given her this incredible man and that she calls him her husband.

"Yeah, I'm fine," she replied while extending her hand to take his.

"Pretty tough in there. She's doing really great, though. All that prepping paid off."

"Yeah, I'm proud of her. She's a tough cookie. And she's ready for the cross-exam, thanks to you."

Because they were professionals in a professional setting, Mia suppressed the urge to pull him close and sample his tongue. She wanted nothing more than to taste his juicy lips right there under the wooden canopy. Instead, she squeezed his hand allowing her fingers to softly stroke his palms. There was something about her beau that was so ridiculously attractive. Mia would find herself wanting to slip into a closet with him even in the worst of times.

"Don't start none. Won't be none," replied Darren fully aware that those subtle strokes always led to happy endings.

Mia winked at him playfully before changing the subject. "Babe, we should adopt."

"What?"

"I know we've talked about this before and you're happy with mentoring the kids at your camp, but I want to see you crawling on the floor playing with our child again." Scooting off of the ledge and standing in front of Darren, she continued enthusiastically. "I want to tag-team diaper changes and potty training with you. I want to rock-paper-scissors with you for the 2:00 a.m. cries. Sweetheart, we have so many gifts and so much love to give and selfishly, Babe - I want to be a mom again. We could be so good − ."

Professional decorum be damned. Darren pulled her into his powerful excited embrace and planted a joyful kiss on his wife's lips. He wasn't sure how it was possible, but he'd managed to fall in love with her all over again.

"I love you." That's all he could muster.

Moments later, Elaine was again placing her hand on the bible swearing to tell the truth. The prosecutor apologized for asking her to return to that tiny bedroom but reminded her that the jury needed to understand the heinousness that the defendant in the orange jumpsuit was capable of.

"Elaine, before the recess, you testified that you thought Max was leaving following the attack. Did he?"

"No."

Elaine told the jury that she'd watched in horror as Max chopped and snorted cocaine, before turning his fully erect attentions back to her. She told the courtroom that all she really recalled about the subsequent assault was its sheer brutality. Max had been close to climaxing for a second time when mercifully, headlights pulled into the driveway. Knowing that that night's callousness had come to an end, Max reluctantly withdrew and slithered out of the bedroom's side window.

The Prosecution then called Marty to the stand. During his exhaustive testimony, he disclosed that upon returning to the home, he and his friends initially assumed that Max and Elaine had left. About twenty minutes later, he had to relieve himself and headed down the hall to the tiny bath. It was then that he noticed his bedroom door – which had been closed when they'd left – was now open. Marty had found Elaine on his bed naked and unable to speak or move.

Marty's anguish was apparent to all as he revealed his awareness of two prior allegations levied against Max when he left Elaine at the house to go on the food and booze run. He confessed through tears that he'd almost told his friends to go without him, but he didn't. Marty just didn't want to believe that his brother, though pompous and insufferable, was capable of those things.

But when he saw the defenseless young woman, he knew the other students were telling the truth and while Elaine couldn't tell him who her attacker was, he knew Max was to blame. Marty released ten thousand years of self-imposed guilt as he cried on the stand divulging that he still felt responsible for what happened to Elaine because deep down, he knew his older brother was a deviant.

Though a warrant had been issued for Max's arrest, Elaine ultimately opted not to press charges. She'd convinced herself that this happened as a result of her "stupidity" and while Ramon, Marty, and the detectives all tried to convince her otherwise, Elaine decided to move on. She and Ramon left California two days later. Nonetheless, her allegation and the subsequent subpoena were the final straws fundamentally leading to Max's expulsion from the university.

Six weeks later, Ramon found himself desperately trying to console Elaine after her third positive pregnancy test. This was years before they'd ever thought of getting married or having children. Guilt ridden, Ramon vowed that if Elaine chose to keep the child, he would be there and love this baby as his own. It was Ramon who'd named Mia and in the early years, it was him who nurtured and loved on Mia. Elaine admitted that it took three years to stop seeing Mia as a constant reminder of that life-altering evening in California.

She even revealed during the trial that while she and Ramon married not long after they learned of the pregnancy, they did not consummate the marriage until a few years later. This was mostly because Elaine needed time to heal, but also because they had planned to hold off on sex for several more years anyway. Their goal had been to finish school, get good jobs, travel, and save lots of money first.

"The Prosecution rests, your Honor."

Mia was thankful to hear those words. They signaled the end of grueling arguments and hopefully meant that their family had seen the last of Maxwell Worthy. While she wouldn't have wished these circumstances on anyone, she was thankful for the strength to endure. She was also grateful to finally have answers to the questions that had nagged her for years. As ugly as the truth was, everything now made sense to Mia. The age gap between her and Mari, her being such a daddy's girl early on, the birthmark on her shoulder, her resemblance to Marty's girls — all explained.

CHAPTER 31:
In a Word – RENEWAL

"**S**HE'S ABSOLUTELY BEAUTIFUL," complimented Eddie Carpenter, flashing his famous crooked smile while admiring little Christina. These days, he was simply known as Eddie since his retirement earlier in the year. While, ultimately, he was found to have had no wrongdoing in discharging his firearm years earlier, the investigation led to murmuring and unnecessary questions from the media. Eddie had been eligible for retirement for several years before the Weeboy Manor event but continued on the bench due to his love for Lady Justice. Nowadays, when he's not hunting or fishing, he can be found contributing to the pro-bono branch of Washington, Worthy & Wilford.

"Thank you, Sir," replied Darren earnestly. Even though they'd begun bonding over the last few years, Darren could never bring himself to call his esteemed friend by his first name. It was always Sir or Judge. Never Eddie.

There were scores of visitors now that little Chrissy was here. Everyone wanting to offer their congratulations and show their support for this beautiful young family. Elaine, was also now fully at peace.

A few months had passed since the trial and, she was still reveling in Max's sentence to eighty years for her rape and that of three other women, including Rhonda Horn, WW&W's former Research Analyst. The sentences were imposed consecutively to his twenty-five years for Randy and Mari's attacks and the incident at Weeboy.

Mia noticed Elaine's new lease on life. Her mom could finally breathe and enjoy herself now that this was behind her. For Elaine, there were no more secrets. Gone were the days of looking over her shoulder and scanning the crowds wondering when Max would show up. She'd been freed from worrying about being outed to Mia and the kids. It was all over. She could now just be Elaine – mom, wife, business partner, and best of all, Ma-Ma.

Marty had also been given a second chance. With no possibility of parole, Max would rot in prison. Ramon and Elaine had assured him that he was not responsible for what happened and that they harbored no ill will towards him. After all, he had become a pseudo protector of Mia – the ultimate silver lining. Marty revealed that he was oblivious to the possibility initially. True, there was an inexplicable connection to her, which he chalked up to his instinct for recognizing good and talented young people. He'd been determined to nurture and develop Mia as he had done for Darren.

Marty liked Mia from the start and while he did notice interesting resemblances, it wasn't until one of their late-night discussions when she'd talked about her parents that he started thinking. He'd heard rumors that the girl he'd helped that evening all those years earlier had become pregnant. Could her parents have possibly been the same Ramon and Elaine?

Not long after that after-hours discussion, Trinity, Marty's youngest daughter, mentioned that she and Mia had similar marks on their shoulders. Dread crept into his heart because that was actually genetic to the Worthy family. His grandma, great aunt, and great grandma all borne some type of birthmark on their shoulders.

When Mia posted her graduation photo with Elaine and Ramon smiling proudly at her side on her shelf at the office, he knew it was true. He remembered Elaine's toothy smile when she'd first come to the house and while he'd never seen Ramon smile during that dark time in California and he didn't wear specks thirty years ago, Marty never forgot his face. Its anguish had been etched into his consciousness.

Marty confessed that he'd made it his mission at that moment to keep Max away from Mia. He'd used Max's outburst at WW&M years earlier as the perfect ruse. Though unconcerned with safety, a restraining order was assurance that he wouldn't run into Mia at the office. His heart completely sank when he heard that Max had run into her with his girls at Hershey Park.

Shamicka C. Toney

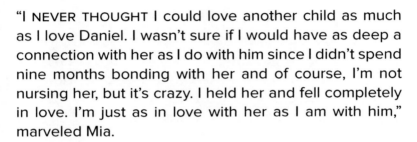

"I NEVER THOUGHT I could love another child as much as I love Daniel. I wasn't sure if I would have as deep a connection with her as I do with him since I didn't spend nine months bonding with her and of course, I'm not nursing her, but it's crazy. I held her and fell completely in love. I'm just as in love with her as I am with him," marveled Mia.

"It doesn't matter if she shares your blood or not, that's your baby girl. She's gonna steal your heart a little more each day," replied Ramon all too knowingly as he hugged his daughter and the two admired Darren tenderly cradling and already doting on the adorable little one fully clad in her first Steelers' jersey. They smiled as Sugar and Ray curiously admired their new baby sister.

Just then, a conversation that she'd had with Dr. Paxton years earlier came to mind. "One day soon, Amia Wilford, you discover the covering that is on your life. I know you can't see it now, but God has you."

It was hard to see the light during that dark time, but now it was clear. Her life wasn't just blessed. On that beautiful July day, Mia discovered that her life was indeed covered.

The world was perfect. The house was alive with joy.

Randy and now wife, Melissa, had stopped by with their three-year-old and a new 6-week-old baby boy. He wouldn't have missed congratulating his former coach on the new baby. Mia chatted with Darren's sisters as they refreshed the finger foods.

Just then, Mable turned the corner with Rhonda Horne in tow. She and Elaine hugged meaningfully. After all, they each belonged to a club that neither of them had applied to. Rhonda had come to congratulate Mia and Darren and to wish them well. Mia escorted Rhonda into their den, where the buzz and excitement was.

Marty's oldest daughter, Faith, who'd been away at school in Ohio, curiously greeted Rhonda. The last time she'd seen her was in May at the grand opening of her 2nd bakery and she was almost eight months pregnant. Today, she was clearly no longer expecting, but did not have a baby in tow. Rhonda nixed the silent inquiry instead hugging Darren and Mia.

During the trial, Rhonda recounted inviting Max over for dinner. Her last memory before waking the next morning completely naked was a shared toast to their future. Rhonda didn't feel she could say anything. She knew Max and Marty were estranged but she'd been seeing him behind her boss' back. So, instead of reporting it, she'd saved her stained sheets, packed up what could fit in her vehicle, and moved back home to Ohio.

Rhonda advised the couple that she would always remember them, hugged each of them for an uncomfortable length of time, and abruptly left. The pair acknowledged the oddity but didn't dwell.

"ARE YOU SURE, Mia? Did something happen to it?" Elaine quizzed her daughter. "Maybe her onesies are too tight around there. Try buying her a bigger size and see if it will go away."

"No, Mom. They're not too tight," Mia cried. "I think this is a birthmark on Christina's shoulder. . ."

CHAPTER 32:
In a Word – FAITHFUL

"**S**O, THE REPORTS are in. There is no DNA match between you and Christina," Dr. Mason happily revealed the news to the anxious parents. Mia and Darren who had been formulating a game plan in the event her and Christina's bloodwork shared markers, wept happily at the revelation. Darren kissed his beautiful baby thankful that they wouldn't have to explain why she was raised by her sister but called her Mom.

"The second reports are also in," Dr. Mason continued. Christina is a DNA match to Rhonda." She handed the paperwork to Rhonda who had joined the couple at the provider's office. Darren insisted that they find her after Faith's pregnancy disclosure. He recalled Rhonda's awkward departure and had a hunch. Mia completely agreed, but because their adoption had been closed, they had to be careful in the approach. The pair decided to visit her new bakery under the guise of wanting to try the cupcakes that were the talk of northeastern Ohio.

Rhonda knew when she saw the world's best sleuth AKA, Amia Wilford with Air-Tight, AKA Darren Wilford that the pair had not made the ninety-mile trek simply to sample her maple lemonade and blueberry tarts.

She seated the couple at a corner table and returned with three cups of cinnamon-infused coffee, her newest creation. Once seated, Rhonda implored them to ask their question to which she simply replied, "Yes." She agreed to the DNA test not just for Darren and Mia's benefit, but also so that she could 100% confirm that the baby had in fact been adopted by them. It wasn't that she mistrusted the agency, but she was not there when Chrissy was handed over to the power couple.

"THANK YOU RHONDA." The trio exchanged hugs for a final time waving as she disappeared over the Smithfield Street Bridge to resume her life in Ohio.

"Hey Daddy. Nope, not a match! The birthmark is actually eczema," Mia exclaimed after they left Dr.

Mason's office. "I know! Dr. Mason confirmed that Rhonda is her birth mom and –."

"Told you." added an extra relieved Darren.

"Yeah, you called it," agreed Mia winking at her indescribably amazing husband. "Anyways, Rhonda said she had eczema as a child too," she added with a heart-happy grin while now speaking with both of her relieved parents who had hung back at the condo with Daniel.

"We're on our way to pick up her prescription and we'll be home in twenty minutes," chimed in Darren. The joy in his heart also clearly evident.

En route to the pharmacy, the giddy couple recounted their intimate discussion with Rhonda in the small parking lot of Dr. Mason's office, where Rhonda revealed that she actually had no idea who fathered Chrissy, but she did share that she'd conceived at her lowest point while in Barbados late last year.

"Bless her heart," whispered Mia. "I can't imagine being so lost that you don't care if you live or die," she added referencing the point in their conversation wherein Rhonda revealed that she'd hooked up with multiple men back then hoping that one of them would just kill her and end her misery.

"But God, Babe. You remember what she said when should found out she was pregnant?"

"Yeah. That the breath literally returned to her lungs. Babe she said she felt like her life had purpose again," Mia recalled. The tears from the parking lot were back again. "And what are the odds that Trinity would visit her first shop a few weeks after she found out about the baby? Trinity didn't even know that it was Rhonda's store." Mia raised her hands praise and thanks.

By this time, Darren had pulled the pharmacy, but instead of hopping out to grab the ointment, he steered into a corner spot and joined his wife in celebrating God's hands in action. "Mia, when she said that she'd called Tex's team to track down possible agencies, I almost lost it. You know Tex and his boys always come through.

"And to think, we almost passed on putting our picture in the Waiting Families book 'cuz we didn't want people in our business. We actually waited almost a month before sending Michelle our picture.

"I know," whispered Mia linking that decision to their earlier conversation. "Rhonda would have never found us if she hadn't flipped through the book at her office. Remember she said that Michelle's agency was the fifth one she went to."

Darren shook his head incredulously. "I can't believe we were so worried about keeping our business covered that we almost smothered the blessing." The pair fell silent for the first time since parking behind Dr. Mason's bricked office – only this time, it wasn't out of dread. This time, their soundlessness was in humbled response to yet another timely revelation. They swore to use every moment of their lives from that minute forward as living testimonies.

The recommitted couple then recalled Rhonda's

parting words, "I have never, ever wanted children, and still have no desire. God used Chrissy to rescue me – of that, I have no doubt. He also used me to deliver her to you. My heart is truly at peace. I *know* that this baby is going to be raised in a beautiful God-fearing home and that her cup will always be running over. Besides, she's got the cutest big brother bodyguard." Rhonda smiled earnestly then said simply as she stepped into her Audi, "Enjoy her."

Darren grabbed the prescription and ten minutes later, they were parking in their newly finished garage. Mia stopped Darren from taking Chrissy out of the seat right away. Instead, she hugged him tightly and they stood embracing each other securely. Again, Darren thanked God for His goodness, mercy and favor towards them. He thanked Him for all of the blessings given to their family and before saying their collective 'Amens', as she'd done consistently since the transit bus incident years earlier, Mia prayed for safe travels for everyone – especially Rhonda.

With that, the blessed pair scooped up their precious baby girl and headed inside delighting in the gleeful shrieks of their little boy followed closely by the cheers of both their families.

In Two Words – The End

About the Author

*S*HAMICKA TONEY IS a compassionate and fun-loving woman of faith who has always strived to live life out loud. When she isn't penning drama-infused love stories, you can find Shamicka immersed in adventure, interior design or working out. She is a consummate professional who loves mentorship, volunteering, and surrounding herself with strong, positive women.

As a creative writer, her passion is giving readers – especially those of faith – something new and fresh to enjoy. Her engaging heartfelt works are soaked in the joys and pains of reality with equal doses of inspiration, life lessons and faith interwoven throughout. Above all else, she enjoys creating as many beautiful memories as humanly possible while traveling and spending quality time with her wonderful husband and incredible children.